Step out for a Saturday night at *The Q*—the small town gay bar in Appalachia where the locals congregate. Whose secret love is revealed? What long-term relationship comes to a crossroad? What revelations come to light? The DJ mixes a soundtrack to inspire dancing, drinking, singing, and falling in (or out) of love.

This pivotal Saturday night at *The Q* is one its regulars will never forget. Lives irrevocably change. Laugh, shed a tear, and root for folks you'll come to love and remember long after the last page.

I0590598

THE Q

Rick R. Reed

A NineStar Press Publication

www.ninestarpress.com

The Q

Printed in the USA

ISBN: 978-1-64890-197-3

First Edition, February, 2021

Also available in eBook, ISBN: 978-1-64890-196-6

WARNING:

This book contains sexual content, which may only be suitable for mature readers. Depictions of domestic abuse, infidelity, death, and suicidal ideation.

For my sister Melissa, who helped inspire this book, whether she knows it or not. See you at Mountaineer with corn starch in hand, little sis.

"The sky grew darker, painted blue on blue, one stroke at a time, into deeper and deeper shades of night."

—*Haruki Murakami, Dance Dance Dance*

Dear Reader,

I began writing *The Q* early in 2020. At that time, I had no idea our world would be gripped in the midst of an unprecedented pandemic. I wanted to tell the story of a little gay bar in the foothills of the Appalachian Mountains (where I grew up, incidentally) and how it was a gathering place for the LGBTQ+ folks who lived in the tristate area (Ohio, Pennsylvania, and the Northern Panhandle of West Virginia). I was committed to telling the bar patrons' stories through one fateful Saturday night. During that night, relationships would begin, some would end, some people would have surprising revelations, and others would realize that, although they thought they might not be happy, they actually had just what they needed to make them so.

And then came the pandemic. As I was writing the book, I was confronted with how to truthfully write a story about a bar where people would be dancing, flirting, kissing, hooking up, drinking and more. To tell these stories, I struggled with how to incorporate the "new normal" of social distancing, mask-wearing, and sanitation.

It didn't work. I thought if I tried to make the story true to our present-day reality, the book would become more about a pandemic than what I wanted it to be—a glimpse into the lives of several people who gathered at the same spot on a regular basis.

So I went with an alternate reality, a world where the pandemic didn't yet exist. I hope you will indulge this flight of fancy as you read, and remember that the most important truths therein are really about life and love.

Thanks for reading *The Q*. If the book has a long shelf life, it's my hope that future readers won't even think about how it was written during the midst of the worst health crisis most of us have ever witnessed.

In the end, this book, just like the bar it portrays, is an escape from everyday reality.

Rick R. Reed

July 2020

Prologue

The Quench Room

First, no one ever called it the Quench Room. To its patrons, it was just the Q. Most of them weren't even aware of its proper name. You wouldn't find it on a sign or in neon. Many—gay, straight, and otherwise inclined—were certain the Q stood for *Queer*. Some saw it as an affirming name, reclaimed from those who'd hurl it to wound. Others whispered it, snickering, rolling eyes.

Second, unless you knew what you were looking for, you'd drive right by the Q, not thinking its sad, nondescript exterior housed much of anything. Lonely and forgotten on a stretch of country road, the Q lay just outside the blink-and-you'll-miss-it town of Hopewell, West Virginia. Housed in a squat, gray cinder block building, the Q had no front door—patrons entered through a chipped red-painted door off the gravel parking lot in the back. The single window out front, long and rectangular, was black tinted so passersby couldn't see inside. For those who came to the Q on the down low, the tinted glass provided a measure of privacy and security.

The Q's nearest neighbors were an auto-body shop called, charmingly, Gomer's, and, down the road just a bit, a no-name bait and tackle shop, open only in summers, for those fishing on the nearby Ohio River.

The Q didn't look like a place where people celebrated.

It didn't appear to be an establishment where people hooked up, hoping for a raunchy one-night stand or dreaming of a lifetime commitment—and everything in-between. A casual glance would never inspire the idea that the Q was a place for socializing, dancing, and drinking.

No one driving by would have imagined this one-story building rising up out of a weed-choked gravel lot was the origin of so many love affairs, failed and sometimes—rarely—successful. Who would want to meet their beloved in such a sad, little shack? Why, it didn't even possess a tin roof...rusted.

And yet, the Q was *the* gathering spot for this little rural area's LGBTQ+ folks, especially those not inspired enough to make their way up the river to the bright lights and fancy bars of Pittsburgh. Pittsburgh, for a lot of the Q's patrons, might as well have existed on another planet.

The Q was open only on Thursday, Friday, and Saturday nights, although Saturday was the busiest. Then, the parking lot was crowded with pickup trucks and various sedans, coupes, and compacts, mostly older and none even remotely close to luxury vehicles. On Saturday nights, only the early birds got parking spots in the lot. If you showed up later, you parked alongside the road and prayed you didn't get sideswiped while inside imbibing and hoping, perhaps, for a special love connection.

Windows down, people driving by on a Saturday night might hear strains of muffled music filtering out— thumping bass, '80s disco tunes going way back to Sylvester and Prince and right up to Lady Gaga and Beyonce, popular line dances, and even some hardcore rock and roll from the likes of ZZ Top, Aerosmith, and maybe even Iron Maiden.

The Q's patrons traveled from the little towns scattered throughout this poor area in the foothills of the Appalachians. They came from upriver in Pennsylvania, across the river in Ohio, and, of course, from right here in the Northern Panhandle of West Virginia. Driving along potholed roads in dusky dusk or navy-blue twilights, you might spy the golden eyes of a fox peeking out from underbrush lining either side of the road.

When you arrived at the Q, though, and stepped through its red-doored portal of a Saturday night, the contrast was almost startling. What, outside, was grim and depressing became magical inside. Voices murmuring, ice clinking in glasses, fairy lights above the big mirror behind the bar, the crack of pool balls, laughter, and maybe, Gloria Gaynor optimistically telling the world she would survive.

And somehow, you knew you would too.

If only for a few hours.

Part One

Raise Your Glass

Chapter One

Hey Bartender!

Mary Louise hated the term fag hag.

It was demoralizing, conjuring up an image of an older woman, heavyset, with too much makeup and hair that was too big. She would be sitting at home with her two cats, Will and Grace, drinking Cosmos alone and streaming *Queer as Folk* or *Queer Eye* while she waited for one of her gay male friends to call to shape and determine the extent of her social life. She'd maybe drink a little too much and laugh a little too loud. She'd play wingperson and watch wistfully from the sidelines as her cohorts paired off for an evening, a week, a month, or a lifetime. She'd tell her friends and family who'd never darkened the threshold of a gay bar that she liked going to them because she didn't get hit on by predatory losers and she could let her hair down.

She knew the stereotype because for many years she'd been it—well, maybe not exactly, but close enough to make her cringe at the memory.

Sure, she still owned cats (or they her, far more likely), who were Siamese and *not* named Will and Grace, but Harry and Sally. Her hair had *never* been big and her idea of great TV was streaming the *Golden Girls* on Hulu. "Okay, so that's a little gay," she heard Sophia saying in the back of her mind. Her drinking taste leaned much more toward beer or a nice glass of whiskey, neat.

She'd broken free of being the wingwoman to the various gay men she befriended. She'd gotten rid of the idea that her happiness depended on a man, gay or otherwise.

She still laughed too loud and probably always would. One of her friends, Mort, delighted in acting out a scene with her from *Who's Afraid of Virginia Woolf* when she let loose with one of her ear-splitting laughs. He'd accuse her of braying, and she'd respond, in her best Elizabeth Taylor, "I don't bray," and then command him to make her another gin and tonic. He always would comply and would sheepishly respond, "All right. You don't bray."

Mort had been gone since 1992, when AIDS took him at the tender age of twenty-eight. Mary Louise still missed him and kept a picture of the two of them, taken while on vacation in Provincetown, a year before Mort was diagnosed. She'd look at that photograph of the two of them, arms slung around each other on Commercial Street, and her eyes would well with tears, even though it had been close to thirty years since Mort had passed in an AIDS ward in a Pittsburgh hospital with only Mary Louise at his side. That loss still was tragic, not only because of Mort's tender age, but because he was so alone. His partner, Nate, and his folks in Shippingport had abandoned him, the former claiming he couldn't stand to see him *this way* and the latter voicing concerns that they might catch the virus. *He was your son!* She'd wanted to scream at the parents. *He needed your arms around him. He needed you to see him. He was your lover!* she'd say to Nate. *His dying and death wasn't about you and your fragile feelings.*

Mary Louise hoped there was a special place in hell waiting for all three of them.

She'd watched many of her friends succumb to the virus before protease inhibitors came onto the scene, turning what was a death sentence into a somewhat manageable condition. She'd never stop mourning the loss of so many beautiful men.

When the fallout from all this was over, for all practical purposes, Mary Louise found herself bereft of friends. That's when she decided to pack up and move back to her home town of Hopewell, where her mom and two sisters still lived. There was comfort in coming home to a place where her roots were deeply embedded, even if the area was blighted with poverty. It was still some of the most beautiful countryside Mary Louise could imagine.

Chicago had suddenly seemed too big and, at the same time, paradoxically empty. There were so many reminders—the Boystown strip along Halsted, the Baton Club on Clark, the Swedish restaurant Ann Sather next to the Belmont L stop—all of these places and so many more held more painful memories than she could count, even if they had the power to make her smile and laugh. She figured time and distance would transform the painful memories into joyous ones.

But each recollection of a night of drunken revelry out with her boys or a bleary-eyed brunch the morning after, were a hot touch to her grief, a pain that may have softened, but never went away. Mary Louise was grateful—she'd never willingly give up the hurt. She wanted to hold onto these memories of her boys forever. Despite the fact she *was* a bit of a stereotype and fit the fag hag profile pretty much to a T, the days and nights in Chicago with her circle of gay friends had been some of the happiest days of her life. And she didn't even realize it at the time. Wasn't that always the way?

Hopewell brought a sense of quiet, with its looming tree-covered hills—the foothills of the Appalachians and its position on a winding curve of the mud-brown Ohio River.

Moving back had simplified her life, even if it drained a lot of the bustle and color from it. In Chicago, she never walked alone; the streets, no matter the time of day or night, were always busy. In Hopewell, she could wander and never bump into anyone.

It was her mom, at eighty-six, who needed her help with things like shopping, cooking, running errands, and chauffeuring her to doctor's appointments. Old Trudy, as she and her sisters referred to her behind her back, refused to move in with one of them, or God forbid, the assisted living facility up the road in Newell. Trudy always said, "I live alone because I like it. They say money is the root of all evil, but the truth is it's people."

Mom got by with her girls. And Mary Louise, even as she sometimes got nostalgic for the bright lights and hustle of the big city, knew she was doing the right thing. She'd experienced the Chicago skyline on a clear night, Lake Michigan's blue/aqua/gray waves crashing against the shore, and the vast diversity of people living on its shore, and no one could ever take those memories away.

Even if she was feisty, clearheaded, and mobile, no one knew how much longer Mom would be with them.

At the Q, Mary Louise still could eye the boys, flirt with them, tease them, and play matchmaker in her role as bartender.

Right now, she stood behind the bar in a pair of unflattering black orthopedic shoes. Once upon a time, Mary Louise adored a pair of CFM (come-fuck-me) pumps with four-inch spikes. Oh, how great they made her legs look back in the day! Not that many noticed in hangouts like Sidetrack or Roscoe's.

Now, midfifties, she needed to be comfortable when she was on her feet all night. Her smile depended on it, and thus her tips.

Currently, she waited for the doors to open, which would happen in about an hour. She was blissfully alone. Well, maybe blissful wasn't the right word because all the lights were on as she prepped citrus and olives for drinks, washed glasses, polished the bar, and made sure the bottles behind it were stocked and ready to go.

The overhead lights cruelly stole most of the limited magic the Q possessed. And that was too bad. One of Mary Louise's favorite characters was the tragic Blanche Dubois, from Tennessee Williams's *A Streetcar Named Desire* and one her favorite lines from the show was Blanche's opinion that she didn't want realism, she wanted magic. The shadows, soft lighting, and even the disco ball above the dance floor lent a kind of alchemy to the place, transforming it from run down to a setting where anything could happen, where hope lived.

Just before the doors opened, though, the joint looked tired and sad (as Mary Louise herself often felt). The cinder block walls, painted black, possessed a menacing air, like a dungeon—and not a fun one! The concrete floor, stained, showed its grit and the cracks that ran through it. Even the single long rectangle window at the front appeared dusty. Night pressed in on the tinted glass like a monster, hungry for admittance.

Stop it! Now you're just getting crazy. Mary Louise finished her prep work and allowed herself a moment to sit on the stool she kept behind the bar. It might be her last chance for several hours to relax, if only for a few minutes. She dreaded the coming ache of her feet at evening's end, orthopedic shoes or not.

But, oh, how she looked forward to seeing everyone! Every Saturday night was a party, and she was the hostess with the mostess.

Despite how some of the regulars could try her patience down to its last reserves, it brought her joy to watch the revelers, to serve them, to offer oblivion in a glass or a bottle. Even though her dancing days, mostly, were well behind her, she loved seeing everyone out there, bodies gyrating and spinning. Some were great, others awkward, others downright embarrassing, but to witness them cut loose after a long week was a thing of beauty, no matter their level of expertise or coordination. She especially loved some of the older patrons, who would bring their shakers of corn starch in to sprinkle on the floor, making it easier to slip and slide to the pulsing dance beat.

Gracie, Rose, and Liz were a lesbian trio that she particularly adored. Even though she'd never had much conversation with them, other than to take their drink orders, the three seemed so well-adjusted and happy, despite never once pairing off, as half the bar expected them to do. And Mary Louise, who considered herself a pretty astute observer of human nature, could tell from a mile away that Gracie was in love with Rose. So obvious! Why couldn't Rose see it? Or did she simply not want to? Mary Louise had wondered if maybe they were a throuple, but everyone she talked to about that particular suspicion shot in down. "They're best friends, that's all."

She turned as the door squeaked open. There stood Billy Breedlove, her barback and bouncer when needed (not often) in his usual garb—black combat boots, black cargo pants, and a black T-shirt that appeared to be painted on his beefy physique—looking worried.

Mary Louise was taken a little aback. For one, her breath always did a little catch in her throat when she saw him, accompanied by a skip of a heartbeat. He was a beautiful man with his muscles, his bleached-blond buzz cut, and the tattoo sleeves, wildly colorful butterflies and birds that ran down both arms. The fact that he was unattainable made him even more attractive.

And then she'd chide herself. *That young man is a good twenty years younger than you, if not more. Cougar. Shame on you.*

He'd once told her, when the doors were closed and the lights back on, as they concluded the evening's business and everyone had headed home, that he was a *volcel*.

"What the hell's that?" Mary Louise had asked, mystified.

"I'm an ace," he'd said, only confusing her further.

"Voluntary celibate, asexual," Billy told her. "I'm better off without the nasty, you know. I just don't want it. It would be hard, no pun intended, if it didn't work for me. But honestly, I never think about sex. Call me weird, but it works for me. And that's all that matters."

On hearing those words, she laughed, disbelieving. She fully expected him to laugh, too, maybe slug her in the arm for being gullible. When he didn't join her in her laughter, her heart broke for him because she knew he wasn't kidding. She'd pined with unrequited love for gay men most of her adult life and here was one who was most likely straight. And wouldn't you know it? He'd sworn off sex.

The world was a hopeless place.

He's too young for you anyway.

The second reason Mary Louise was taken aback was from the worry stamped on Billy's face.

"There's been an accident," he called over. "It's bad."

"Oh no." Mary Louise stood. "What happened?"

Chapter Two

Nobody to Love

Nelson DiCarlo wondered, for the thousandth Saturday night, why he didn't stay home.

After all, he had regular cable, Netflix, Hulu, Amazon Prime, and YouTube. He had a fully stocked liquor cabinet and could make himself just about any cocktail he could imagine, from the simple—gin and tonic with a twist of lime—to the exotic—a Pimm's Cup with orange and cucumber slices. His pantry was stocked with chips, cookies, and crackers to go with the cheeses and dips in his fridge.

His dog, Homer, a so-ugly-he's-cute mix of dachshund and poodle, was always ready to cuddle or take a long walk in the night air. So, he couldn't say he was lacking for company. Homer was short on judgment, long on love, and as long as Nels was paying attention, the dog never got bored. If Nels's attention did stray, the dog reeled him back in by covering his face with kisses.

No, really, there was no reason why he, at sixty-two years old, should be getting ready to go out to a bar on Saturday night. Really, he needed to simply accept his lot and stay in, go to bed early like the old man he was.

Nearly entirely banished were the dreams that being out at the Q—the only gay bar in his little one-horse town of Hopewell, West Virginia—would conjure up a man who'd be everything Nels dreamed of: a passionate lover, a faithful companion, a best friend forever. He even held out little reason to believe the conversations he'd have with the same folks he saw every Saturday at the Q would be any different or more exciting than they had been on any other Saturday night, dating back years.

He had no reason to think that, even if he'd given up all hope for a Mr. Right to come along on his white horse, he would meet a Mr. Right Now. There were a few of those in his past, but none lately. Not for a long time... So long, in fact, that Nels no longer pined for a physical connection with another man.

So why go out?

It was routine. It was a bore.

He was old. And so, so tired.

Yet, here he found himself, in the tiny blue-and-yellow ceramic tile bathroom of the house he'd grown up in—the one he'd inherited from his mom when she passed from lung cancer seven years ago—shaving in front of the medicine cabinet mirror.

It was funny, how he sometimes glimpsed the man he once was in that mirror, especially when half of his wizened face was hidden by Barbasol shaving cream.

If he squinted just right, he could look back in time and see the man he'd once been, hidden in the depths of the glass. He'd been handsome, what Mom would call a head-turner. On the shorter side, at five feet, eight, Nels had been solidly packed with effortless muscle and good definition. Firm pecs. Bulging biceps. Thick, black wavy hair and eyes so dark the pupils got lost in the irises. A perpetual five o'clock shadow that highlighted, rather than hid, the sharp angles and planes of his face, a contrast to his cupid's bow lips. People, men mostly, used to tell him he should be a model.

That young buck hidden in the mirror was forever mistaken for being younger than he actually was. In his twenties, he was always asked for an ID. When he was in his thirties, everyone imagined he was in his twenties. In his forties, people guessed thirties. Even in his fifties, folks would guess mid- to late-forties and they were always surprised when Nels corrected them, because he never lied about his age. It was always a delight to get the compliments, "I never would have guessed!" "What's your secret?" And that dreaded left-handed compliment, "You look great—for your age."

And then, suddenly, and without warning, he looked his age. The revelation crept up quietly—and fast.

Nels would guess it happened around the time he hit his late fifties, when the hair at the top of his head had thinned so much that more scalp than hair showed, when the hair above his ears and at the back of his head, now shorn short, turned mostly salt. When tufts began sprouting stubbornly from his ears and growing on his back. When his waistline went from a reliable thirty-two to thirty-three and then thirty-four. Nels wouldn't buy a pair of Levi's bigger than that, no matter how tight they were. And he didn't even want to consider the bags under his eyes or the lines across his forehead and around his mouth. They called those latter ones laugh lines, but Nels DiCarlo wasn't laughing. No, he wasn't in the least amused.

That young guy, he was told more than once at the Q, back in the days when it was a secret place and one had to be buzzed in the door, that he could have his pick of any of the men in the bar...anytime.

And he did. Pick and pick and pick—a kid in a candy store. Rarely did anyone refuse Nels's attention. They came home with him or he with them. Sometimes they lasted more than a night or a couple dates. Some, like Roger Baines, lasted years, despite his having a wife tucked away across the Ohio River. Roger was forever promising to leave Betsy, once she finished her degree and found a job, or once their daughter, Joy, was grown and out of the house. Nels had wasted his twenties on the loser, years he'd never get back.

How many Christmases had Nelson sat alone, hoping Roger would at least call him to wish him a merry one? Would it have been so hard to at least pick up the telephone?

Every man Nelson had fallen in love or lust with had turned out to be a disappointment.

How could his odds have been so bad? What had he done to make him so unlovable? He'd always been able to rely on his looks and now those were fading fast.

Would someone even look twice at him these days?

These were questions he pondered in the middle of the night, when the eaves groaned in response to the lonely wind and Homer snored lightly, curled up under the covers in the crook of Nels's knees.

For a long time, he'd relied on his handsomeness to connect him to men and, indeed, to the rest of humanity. His attractiveness made him *visible*. People *saw* him. Whether those same looks inspired jealousy, intrigue, or passion, they were reliable. He could count on them. He could bank on the hope they provided.

And when they began to fade, Nelson started to wonder who he really was. Who was the guy behind the pretty face? Was there any substance there? Or had he been all gloss and veneer, with nothing substantial behind the pretty?

He took his looks for granted until they were gone. He'd grieve the loss if he didn't know, deep in his heart, time caught up to everyone. At least in that regard, he wasn't alone—small comfort.

Once his age was writ large across his features, he became the watcher instead of the watched.

On his best days, he'd tell himself the invisibility, this cloak he'd never chosen, was liberating. He could do what he wanted, say what he wanted, and no one gave a damn.

But really. Was being unseen so wonderful?

Finished shaving, he rinsed the lather from his face and slapped on some Old Spice aftershave, the same kind his dad once wore, before a heart attack took him at the age Nels was now. He often wondered if his sixty-second year would end the same as his father's—rising one morning, expecting a normal day, blissfully unaware that there were only a few minutes remaining before dropping dead on the bathroom floor. In his mind, Nels could still hear the thud of his father hitting the floor as Nelson ate his Cheerios in the kitchen downstairs. He shuddered as he remembered calling, "Dad!" and desperately trying to push open the door, which was blocked by his father's body.

He shook his head to clear it of the memory—best as he could.

Nelson's eyes were the same, though, staring back. At least they were still young, vibrant, glistening with a young man's hopes and dreams. Although Nels wasn't much to look at anymore, it was these never-aging eyes that made him repeat the same routine every Saturday night because...

Because...

Well...*hope.*

Wasn't it Emily Dickinson who said hope was the thing with feathers? Nelson recalled seeing a drag queen once at a bar in Pittsburgh who called herself Hope Winters and she bounced on to the stage of the crowded little bar in an outfit of rainbow-colored feathers affixed to her six-foot-four, three-hundred-pound frame.

The crowd at the Q was always the same, but there *could* come a time when someone new walked in. Someone maybe close to Nelson's age, for he didn't care any longer about hot young studs; he wanted only a companion, someone to hold, with whom to share holidays and ordinary days. Of course, he wanted a man with whom he could celebrate life's ups, but also a man who realized what the downs were and knew ways to make them better, even if that might only be a pot of homemade minestrone on the stove on a rainy Saturday night and *Imitation of Life*, the Lana Turner version, queued up in the DVD player.

If he missed a Saturday night at the Q, he could miss that man who might change Nelson's life forever.

What was that old saying? Don't leave five minutes before the miracle?

Eternal optimist, he could think of himself. Or, when he drove home in the wee small hours of the morning, he could believe he was one of those for whom the definition of insanity was invented: *doing the same thing over and over and expecting a different outcome.*

At least by being optimistic, he allowed for change, even as the possibility seemed to grow more and more remote with each passing Saturday night.

He shrugged and went into his bedroom to get dressed.

Homer watched from his place on a mound of pillows at the head of the bed as Nelson tossed out clothing options for his evening. Landing on the blue-and-white quilt were a couple pairs of jeans (one dark, pressed, and crisp, and the other worn, faded, with the knees just beginning to fray), a black Grace Jones T-shirt, a white Iron City beer T-shirt, a button-down blue-and-white shirt with small checks, followed by various socks and pairs of underwear. The latter represented hope—there were camo bikinis, plaid boxers, and a pair of plain black boxer briefs.

"What are the odds of someone laying their hands on these?" He held up the boxers, showing them to Homer. "Or these?" He dropped the boxers and grabbed the bikinis.

Homer cocked his head but kept his own counsel.

"No comment, eh? What good are you?"

Homer lowered his head, farted, and closed his eyes. He was asleep within seconds.

Nels eyed the dog for a moment, dropping the hand that had held the bikini briefs aloft to his side. *You've got the right idea, buddy. I should curl up beside you and go to sleep, too, just like any sensible old dog.* Nelson moved close to Homer, and his hand hovered above the dog's head, but he didn't pet. No need to disturb his slumber. No reason one of them shouldn't have a satisfying experience in bed tonight.

Nelson laughed. He decided on the dark jeans with the button-down. He sat on the bed to don his socks and black Chuck Taylors, his signature shoe since he was a teenager, back when he played basketball in his backyard and even dated girls.

He smiled and shook his head. *Seems like a lifetime ago. A different person.*

And yet, his youth, paradoxically, seemed like it had happened only recently, the passing years compressed into a neat little box, almost as though they'd never been.

Nelson snagged his wallet and keys from the dresser and debated whether he should wear his faded denim jacket or not. It was early summer, the night was warm, and the jacket, flattering as he might have thought it, would be a nuisance.

He decided to leave it in the closet. If he was chilly when he emerged from the bar later tonight, well, his car heated up quickly. And who knew? Maybe, just maybe, there'd be a warm someone on the seat beside him.

Lord. It's been so long.

He headed out, passing through the living room toward his front door. As he went by the little oak secretary desk near the front, he laid his hand for a moment on a silver-framed portrait of his mom. In it, she was young and beautiful, only eighteen, wearing a black, low-cut dress and her signature cameo. Dark curls surrounded her face. Her eyes, even in this old black-and-white portrait, sparkled.

Her smile was the one thing that had never changed, even as the years passed, even as her cancer had taken hold. It was always warm, always inviting. It was a smile that made one take notice and feel like she was just damn happy to see you. It made Nels feel like he was the only person she saw.

"G'night, Mom," he whispered. Tears rose to his eyes for just a moment and he pressed against his eyes to prevent them from falling. "I hope I still have your smile."

As he opened the door, letting in the murmur of crickets, he heard his mom's voice behind him. He didn't dare turn to look back for fear of breaking the spell.

"Of course, you have the same smile, Nels! You lucky man. You got my good looks—and your father's, may he burn in hell." She laughed and her voice was velvety, deep. "Nels, understand one thing. Life, as I see it, is rolling down a hill. When you're a kid, it's all fun and dizziness. Giggles and sunshine.

"But as you grow older, the hill gets steeper, rougher, not so much grass, more rocks, pebbles, dirt. And then there's that damn cliff at the end!

"You don't see that until you're almost ready to fly over the edge—"

Her voice stopped abruptly, and Nelson still listened, yearning for the sound of that honey-warm voice, when he realized he wasn't really hearing it at all. He'd made it up, of course, out of desire, out of memory, out of grief.

Still, he thought, it was a comfort.

And a warning.

Chapter Three

The Stranger

He'd landed at Pittsburgh International Airport only a few hours ago, on a flight from New York's LaGuardia. Even though the travel time was only a little more than an hour, Pittsburgh seemed a world away from where he'd grown up, the Upper West Side of Manhattan, at 83rd and Riverside.

He didn't like to think about that home anymore.

He'd grown up in a five-story graystone building with a cramped elevator, nosy neighbors, and views of other buildings and water towers. There were two saving graces to his building. The first was the rooftop, for which his family's condo had exclusive rights. Up there, one could look out at the Hudson River and see easily across its water to Hoboken, New Jersey. As Riccardo had grown, he'd helped his dad with the little garden up there, coaxing herbs, tomatoes, and Swiss chard from the earth. They'd cook out and watch the sunset on summer evenings.

The second saving grace was that this is where he'd grown up with his parents. His father had been, once upon a time, an opera singer and had performed around the world, mainly with minimalist composer Philip Glass. Toward the end of his life, he taught voice and acting at NYU. His mother, older than his dad by a decade, had been a successful romance novelist, cranking out at least four bodice rippers every year for more than twenty years. It was this work, frowned upon by their cultural elite friends, that had made them relatively wealthy.

And now, both were gone, not from old age, cancer, or heart disease, but from a car accident on the Long Island Expressway that claimed both of them suddenly. He admired his parents' love for each other so much that it was a small comfort they left the earth together, quickly, completely, and, he fervently hoped, painlessly and without fear.

Their passing had been last winter at the start of the new year.

They never got to see him get married on Valentine's Day. And they would never know their grandchild, a little boy already named Tate, waiting to make his way into this heartbreaking and chaotic world.

The news he'd discovered, quite innocently, just over a week ago, had led him to Pittsburgh, which was just down the Ohio River from the small town in West Virginia, Hopewell, his ultimate destination.

Once he'd left Pittsburgh's airport, he piloted his rental car, a black Kia Soul, along a winding two-lane road lined with modest homes, copses of maple trees just beginning to bud, yellow forsythia bushes, and an ever-darkening sky. When he started out, that sky was a pale-blue canvas, dabbed with strands of white cloud. But as he got closer to the West Virginia state line, the sky served up a sunset he'd always remember—layers of gray, lavender, and tangerine—on what he hoped would be an auspicious, life-changing night.

There were glimpses of the slow-moving greenish brown river as he proceeded along. He saw cooling towers, lights blinking, and steam emerging from their tops as he passed the border between Pennsylvania and West Virginia.

He'd never dreamed he'd find himself here, in the foothills of the Appalachians, the tree-covered mounds towering over him, the air fresh coming in through the car vents. He was a city boy, born and raised, and had seldom, in his thirty-odd years, ventured far from New York. There never seemed to be a reason, when the city offered almost everything his heart could desire.

And then, one of those simple DNA tests he bought off Amazon changed everything. A few drops of spit, a padded postage-paid envelope, and voila—life morphed with the simple gesture of opening an envelope and consulting a website. He'd done the test not because he was curious about his own origins, but because he wanted to be able to pass along this information to his new son.

It had never mattered to him before that he was adopted.

He had always believed that your *real* parents were the ones who raised you, clothed you, fed you, sung and read you to sleep, sat through boring school programs, listened to your sorrows and your joys, and who simply loved you as their very own—because you *were*.

And now, as the sky darkened fully into night, he needed to stop. He pulled over at the side of the road and rolled down his window, letting the chill night air and the sounds of wind and crickets in.

What caused him to pull over was an epiphany. He had the oddest sense of homecoming. He'd tried to discount it. After all, he'd never been to this part of the country, even though it was only six or so hours away from New York.

Yet he felt he was coming home just the same.

Can home be in two places? he wondered.

Am I setting myself up for a colossal disappointment?

Unshakeable, though, this sense of both returning and hurtling toward something significant.

He shook his head, told himself to be practical, restarted the car, and pulled back out onto the road. His GPS screen told him he was less than an hour away from the motel he'd booked.

And his own heart told him he was less than two hours away from meeting his destiny, whatever that turned out to be.

"I can only see as far as the beams of my headlights," he reminded himself as he eased up on the gas pedal.

Chapter Four

The Three Bells

Gracie Fuentes lit a fresh Newport off the butt of the last. She exhaled a cloud of smoke into the air above her head. Pushing back the recliner, she reminded herself to relax, that it was Saturday, that she wasn't slinging hash at the diner across the river in Summitville, but it was hard.

Her best friends, Liz Sgro and Rose Dalrymple, were getting ready to head out for the usual Saturday night revelry at the Q—and their silliness knew no bounds. What might have been endearing to Gracie at one time was now annoying. She wanted to stay home, curl up with the latest Jazzy Mitchell novel, down an Orange Crush and some salt and vinegar chips...and be in bed by nine.

Alone.

That's what she told herself anyway. And she almost believed it—but she recognized a lie when she saw one, damn it. She was no queen of denial. Gracie was constitutionally unable to lie to herself, although she had to admit she did a pretty good job of bending the truth to conform to her own hopes and fears.

"Honest to Christ, you guys, you act more like a couple of teenyboppers than grown women," she said, words borne up on a cloud of blue-gray smoke.

"Oh, get bent, you old dyke!" Liz cried. "Just because you're a stick-in-the-mud doesn't mean we have to be."

"Yeah!" Rose said with her usual wit. She crossed the shag-carpeted living room of Gracie's double-wide to switch off the TV.

"Hey, bitch! I was watching that."

"Really?" Liz put her hands on her hips. "*The Great British Bake Off*? When did you ever bake anything more complicated than a goddamn brown sugar and cinnamon Pop-Tart?"

"Yeah!" Rose agreed. "And that was probably burnt." She threw back her head and laughed at her own wit, or what passed for it, anyway.

It *was* funny. Rose would never say a mean thing, even in jest, unless Liz was around.

Why is that?

Liz turned to Gracie's ancient stereo system and switched on the receiver. She shuffled through Gracie's CDs and popped an Indigo Girls album in, mumbling, "Who the hell listens to CDs anymore?" When "Closer to Fine" started up, she stood, pleased with herself. She turned to Rose and took her in her arms, spinning her around Gracie's tiny living room and twirling her around with alarmingly good jitterbug moves.

Gracie eyed them with a growing sense of unease.

They're just having fun. It's Saturday night and we're getting ready to go out dancing and drinking, just like we always do. What the hell do you have to be jealous about, anyway? You've known these gals since you were all spring chickens.

And this last thought conjured up Rose at twentysomething. Sweet, naïve, and sometimes stupid Rose, whose heart was bigger than her brain. Gracie had come to realize as she grew older that possession of a big heart was much more appealing in a person that having a big brain.

Gracie took a sip of her drink and closed her eyes. She pictured Rose dancing alone, but with her gaze trained on Gracie with a come-hither look. Rose had been gorgeous in her twenties. She still was, some two decades later, a little thicker around the thighs and hips maybe— but weren't we all?—a few more lines around her eyes and her mouth, but she still had the vibrancy of the girl Gracie had met and befriended at the Q all those years ago. Because her figure was fuller and her face marked by the passage of time, she was somehow even more attractive. Those blue eyes of hers sparkled as they did when they were pups. And Rose's hair, now cropped short in a shoulder-length bob and streaked with gray, continued to cause Gracie to want to run her hands through it, to revel in its silky smoothness. Because, even if it *was* older hair, it was still smooth as a young girl's. Gracie's, on the other hand, was a helmet of gray that she knew she should do something about—color it, find a less-dated cut—but she never seemed to find the time to actually act on it. Gracie went to a barber, for Christ's sake.

Rose was never yours. And she never will be. Be thankful she's your friend. Be even more thankful she never took up with Liz.

Gracie had feared the two of *them* would become a couple for as long as she could remember, way back to when they had all become a trio once upon a time over beers and country line dancing at the Q, when they used to have it on Wednesday nights.

Gracie shook her head. She sometimes wondered why these two had been her friends for so long. What they lacked in charm, they more than made up for in snark and crass behavior that Gracie, in her most honest moments, had to admit was endearing in a perverse sort of way.

And then Gracie burst into laughter because she knew why—they tickled her. They made her laugh. They, damn them to hell, shone a little sunshine into the dreariness that passed for her life.

And these Saturday night rituals, which always ran roughly according the same script, were the highlight of Gracie's week.

Nothing ever changed, except the passage of years marching across their bodies and faces and, for that,

Gracie was grateful. As long as they maintained the status quo, they'd remain the three friends they were. Yes, sometimes, in the darkest hours of an early morning, when Gracie lay alone and tossing in her queen-size bed, she knew the three of them being a trio was insurance against Rose and Liz ever becoming a couple, which she dreaded and expected, like taxes and death.

She never admitted to anyone, least of all Rose, that her biggest longing was for Rose herself. That longing had gone from a youthful lust and imaginings of ravishing Rose's generous form—so womanly, so perfect—to simply thinking of the two of them, curled up together on a Saturday night. Instead of going out, they'd stay in, sitting close on the couch with assorted cats and dogs at their feet, watching old movies on TV—stuff like *Now, Voyager* or *Double Indemnity*. Their bellies would be full of the enchiladas Gracie made for dinner, redolent with tomatoes, oregano, and garlic, and gooey with queso fresco.

"Come on, Gracie! Get off your ass and dance with us!" Liz cried.

And Gracie, despite wanting to push Liz away from Rose (and right out the front door) joined them, a smile on her face and tears in her eyes.

"Are you crying?" Rose asked, her head cocked.

"Ah, it's from those damn Newports. That's all," Gracie replied as she stood back to let Liz twirl Rose. "One of these days, I'll quit."

When the song at last ended, Gracie turned toward her bedroom. "Gotta get ready, try to make myself presentable."

"Good luck with that!" Liz said.

"Hey." Rose gave Liz a playful punch in the arm. "Gracie's beautiful."

And that stopped Gracie in her tracks. Heat prickled her face. *Really? Do you really think so?* Gracie shook her head. *Ah. Rose's kind to everyone. Don't get yourself all worked up.* She hurried from the room, shutting the door firmly behind her.

*

Her bedroom was a shrine to Gracie's past. The furniture had once belonged to her parents, now resting side by side at Mount Peace Cemetery, which overlooked the valley and the twisting brown snake cutting through it, the Ohio River. Maple queen-size bed, dresser, and chest of drawers crowded the little room. Gracie sometimes wondered how the hell the furniture had held up through all of these years, given that it was never expensive—cheap veneer and bought at the big discount furniture outlet over in Youngstown, Ohio when Gracie herself was only about thirteen. Hell, the bed even had the same mattress and box springs it had come with back in the day. Sure, it was lumpy and had a dip where her dad, a big man with a beer belly, had slept, but it was serviceable.

Hanging from the mirror atop the chest of drawers—her mom, a hoopy from down river in West

Virginia called it a *chester drawers*—were dusty Mardi Gras beads in purple, gold, and green thrown Gracie's way from a balcony in the French Quarter twenty-odd years ago. She looked at them as a treasure because they represented a tribute to her, tossed down to her by a steel-haired, but gorgeous older woman in exchange for a flash of Gracie's breasts. Oh, those were the days.

Where does the time go?

Gracie sat on the bed and it creaked and moaned as was its habit these days. Gracie herself was known for creaking and moaning, and not in a good way, in this very bedroom. Pickles, her one-eyed, black-and-white cat, hopped up beside her and butted her arm with her head, purring. The cat was coming up on seventeen soon and Gracie was once again grateful she could still lithely leap from the floor to the bed in one motion. Gracie wished she would age as gracefully as this old gal. She scratched behind her ears, sending up a cloud of cat hair and causing the purring to sound like a semi starting up.

The surfaces of the dresser and chest of drawers bore testimony to Gracie's past. Though she seldom looked at all the photographs, some black and white, some Polaroids, some sun-faded prints from Instamatic cameras, she treasured every one of them because, in rag-tag fashion, they told the story of Gracie's life. Everyone who mattered was included in the little gallery of brass-framed pictures—Grandma and Grandpa, who'd lived down in Follansbee, Mom and Dad on their wedding day. Dad looked petrified and Mom, big and busty in her homemade white dress, looked as though she'd just bagged some elusive wild game. There was Aunt Jackie, Mom's sister, with her flipped collar and fire-engine red lips and nails, always an icon of glamor. Although Gracie was never tempted to emulate Jackie, she always admired her for never having a hair out of place and for never leaving the house without her face on.

And, of course, sprinkled in among all the family photos were pictures of the "girls," Gracie, Rose, and Liz. There they were sunning themselves on the banks of the Ohio, the boom box dating them. And here, they were on a cruise to the Bahamas they all took together one year.

She stood to pick that one up. It was probably the most professional photograph in her collection, taken when they boarded the cruise ship in Miami, back in the early '90s. Taken by the ship's photographer, it memorialized them in that exciting moment in time. Rose, in a bright teal sundress with halter straps that showed off her tan, smiled at the camera, eyes twinkling, blonde hair in a long braid down her back. Liz, standing on one side of her, wearing plaid Bermuda shorts and a white button-down shirt, had her head thrown back in laughter. Gracie'd be damned if she could remember the cause of Liz's mirth.

And Gracie herself, on the other side of Rose, wearing jeans and a black T-shirt, the only one *not* looking at the camera, but at Rose. Her adoring eyes told a tale of unrequited love. Any fool could see it.

She set the photo back on the dresser and moved to her bed. She lay down on it this time, Pickles padding over to curl up beside her. "No, hon, it's not time for bed yet." Gracie petted the cat.

And why isn't it? It's what I really want to do. I can just stay here with Pickles, turn on the TV, and watch old episodes of The Golden Girls *or* Designing Women *on Hulu.*

The idea had its appeal. And why couldn't she simply do what her heart told her was right? If she went to the Q, she'd watch Liz and Rose dance from her bar stool, just like every other Saturday night in recent memory. Gracie was always on the sidelines, but it was her own fault. They were forever motioning her from the dance floor to join them. She knew the blame for being left out lay squarely on her own shoulders. And sometimes, the urge to order a Jack and Coke seized her, just so she'd be uninhibited enough to get out on the crowded dance floor and shake her booty.

Fact was, she simply didn't want to. It was as though some unseen hand had flipped a switch tonight, removing the allure of the Q completely. What she once yearned for, she now dreaded.

Maybe it was time to step away...

Maybe she had finally crossed the line from middle-aged to old. Given up.

She rose from the bed and carefully undressed, depositing her clothes on an old armchair, with a gold-and-brown floral pattern, in the corner of the room. It had once been in her parents' front room. She had a quick vision of Mom in it, crocheting the yellow-and-white throw that still lay at the foot of Gracie's bed.

Naked, she crossed to her closet and pulled out her blue quilted bathrobe and buttoned it up to her neck. She bent to pull out her slippers from under the bed, black-and-white with cat heads at the feet, and put them on.

Now, I'm dressed for a proper Saturday night—for an old lady with a cat.

Gracie chuckled at the thought and found comfort in it. She crossed the room and opened the door. Rose and Liz had stopped dancing and were seated on the couch together. With an inner wince of pain, Gracie thought how good they looked together, how they fit one another—one light, one dark, one smart or at least smart-*ass*, one naïve, gullible, but with a classic heart of gold.

When Gracie entered the room, Liz set down her beer and looked up. Rose turned, too, to peer at Gracie, her head cocked. She might not have been the brightest bulb in the pack, but her intuition was keen. She knew something was up. The robe was a giveaway.

Gracie paused for a moment, gathering together the words she wanted to say. "Ladies, I'm just not feelin' it tonight. You go on without me. I'm going to stay home, draw a bath, and get into bed and finish *You Matter*."

"Is that a book?" Rose asked.

Gracie nodded. "A very good one. I'll loan it to you when I'm done."

Rose nodded, staring at her. "Wait. You're not coming with us?"

Liz's eyebrows came together in concern. "You okay?"

"I'm fine. I'm fine. I had to be honest with myself though. And what I really want tonight is a quiet night at home." *With Rose*, her mind supplied, without being asked. She chuckled. "I'm turning into an old bag. Shoot me if you catch me with a crochet hook in my hands, smelling of moth balls and BENGAY."

Rose and Liz both laughed at that. Liz stood, grabbing her cigarettes from the coffee table and then leaning over to snatch her denim jacket from the recliner. She put it on. To Rose, she said, "I'll wait for you in the truck."

Gracie usually drove them. She was, in fact, their designated driver, because she'd given up drinking when she suddenly realized she was no longer in control of how much, or when, or even what she consumed, *alcoholically* speaking. She'd be sober six years this September.

Rose turned from the closed French door through which Liz had just exited. The sparkle in her eyes had dimmed and her smile had gone AWOL. "Why aren't you coming?"

Ah, honey. Why aren't you staying?

"I just told you, sweetie. I'm tired. Bed, a good book, and Ms. Pickles by my side is all I need tonight."

"Okay."

"How pathetic is that?" Gracie tried for a smile and failed.

Rose crossed the room. She laid a hand on Gracie's shoulder. The touch sent a pulse of electricity through Gracie. She shivered. "Shut up. It's not pathetic. You're not pathetic. Come with us. It won't be the same without you."

Gracie was about to say that she'd been wrong, give her a couple minutes to throw on a pair of jeans and a sweatshirt and she'd be right with them, but then Liz honked on the horn, a loud, annoying, and continuous tone that seemed to go on for at least a minute.

Gracie turned Rose around and pointed her toward the door. She allowed herself to slap the ass she'd always admired. "Go. I'll be okay. Call me in the morning, and we can meet up at the Tea Kettle for breakfast."

Rose headed toward the door. "I'll hold you to that." She opened the door but paused for a moment. She turned her head to regard Gracie over her shoulder. "I wish you were coming."

Gracie's mouth was open to respond when the horn sounded again.

Rose rolled her eyes. "That woman's working my last nerve."

Gracie laughed because the comment was so out of character for Rose. "Mine too, mine too. You guys have a good time. Dance like *everyone's* watching." *Because they are, my sweet, because they are.*

Especially me.

Gracie stood frozen in her living room, listening to the sound of the truck's passenger door slamming, the shift of gears, and, finally, the dying sound of the F-150's engine as it roared away. Even when the sound was gone and silence crept back in, Gracie stayed there for a few long moments until Pickles came in and joined her, purring and doing a figure eight between her calves.

Groaning, Gracie scooped the cat from the floor and hugged her close.

Chapter Five

Keeping the Love Alive

"What are the rules again?" Despite asking the question, Wally turned up the volume for the song playing on the oldies radio station out of Pittsburgh. Dee-Lite's "Groove is in the Heart" took Wally right back to meeting Joel at a Pittsburgh dance bar one hot August night in 1990.

Even after three decades, Wally could still clearly visualize Joel across the dance floor, shirt off, muscles rippling and coated with sweat, dancing alone and not caring—one with the music. Joel was just about the most gorgeous man Wally had ever seen—black curly hair, olive skin, irises so dark you couldn't find a pupil if you tried. Back then, Joel sported a big *Magnum PI* mustache that curled just a bit when he smiled.

It was that very same smile that endowed Wally with the courage to go up and dance with Joel. Normally, Wally would have hugged the wall with his friend, Bobbi Janine, speculating on the dancers, finding them irresistible, or shallow, or "mutton dressed as lamb."

Sometimes, when the drink was making her really mean, as it occasionally did, Bobbi Janine would call out some poor overweight queen as "ten pounds of shit in a five pound bag." Wally would try not to snicker. Bobbi could be so cruel. She was also his best and most loyal pal— Wally suspected her sarcastic wit that often bordered on hateful was a defense, a suit of armor she wore against her loneliness. She was also his next-door neighbor at the apartment building they both lived in, nestled in the downtrodden charm of Pittsburgh's Mexican War Streets. Bobbi Janine had been first to welcome him to the neighborhood, with a couple of joints and a bottle of Jack Daniels in hand. She reminded him of a younger Mrs. Madrigal in Armistead Maupin's *Tales of the City* books.

Bobbi Janine had passed away four years ago from lung cancer at the tender age of sixty-two. He still missed her and their marathon videocassette and, later, DVD binges of truly horrible gay romances and dramas.

Joel turned down the volume on the Mazda's stereo to answer Wally's question which, in his little reverie and trip down memory lane, he'd forgotten. "You ask a question and then turn up the music. Mix your signals much?" Joel snorted.

Wally looked over at him, keeping his smile firmly in place. "We talked about this and I agreed to go along." He was still the handsomest man Wally had ever laid eyes on. Sure, he was now fifty-three instead of twenty-three, but the years had been kind. Joel's dark hair had stayed thick and had morphed into a beautiful silver, which made his dark eyes stand out all the more. Unlike Wally, his frame was lean, although maybe not as muscular. He'd grown into what the kids called a "hot daddy" these days.

"Go along? Seriously?" Joel shook his head and stared for a moment out the side window. Shadows crowded the densely wooded sides of the road. The summer night air coming in through their windows was humid and Wally longed for the day when the heat would have an undercurrent of chill to it, foretelling autumn nights. "Go along?" Joel slowly shook his head. "You bowl me over with your enthusiasm." Joel switched off the radio. "Listen. We don't have to do this if you don't want to. Don't look at as a favor to me."

"You just think it would spice things up a bit?" *But it is a favor to you. I want no part of this.*

"Yes," Joel answered, with patience. "It's not like we're opening up our relationship, for God's sake. It'll be just be a little harmless fun."

Why does it feel like you're rationalizing? Why am I having trouble believing you? Wally stared out at the fireflies winking and dancing in the air. The smell of the river, less than a mile over, rose up.

Harmless? He wasn't so sure about that. He'd been afraid of the little role-playing idea when Joel first proposed it a month or so ago, and he was still afraid of it. And why shouldn't he be? From the time he first met him, Wally had always felt Joel was way out of his league. Wally was a bit of a nerd, who couldn't see worth a damn without his thick-lensed glasses. Unlike his husband, Wally's hair had started thinning when he was in his thirties. Now, all that remained was a salt-and-pepper rim around his shiny pate. And he had a little gut that stubbornly refused to go away no matter what low-carb diet he tried or what exercise he attempted.

From the start, Wally feared someone worthier than he, and a lot sexier, would whisk Joel away. And Wally almost wouldn't blame Joel if he opted for a newer model. Joel's idea to role-play on this particular Saturday night Wally saw as a real threat, despite trying to be supportive.

"Right, harmless." Wally agreed, against his own instincts for self-preservation. He leaned harder against the passenger door.

The idea was for the two of them to go out to the Q, the little gay bar out in the sticks and down river from Pittsburgh, and to pretend each was single. They would also play the roles of not really knowing one another. They'd spend the evening flirting with potential prospects and then, miraculously, well before closing time, end up spying each other from across a crowded room, just like in the movies. Their gazes would lock, albeit shyly. They would then proceed to act as though they were just meeting for the very first time with all the awkwardness and excitement such meetings entailed.

It all sounded good, reasonable even, on paper. But Wally wasn't so certain. He couldn't help but wonder if Joel hadn't a hidden agenda. Maybe this was a ploy to check out a prospective replacement, all the while hiding his intentions in plain sight. Thirty years was a long time to be together. Even though Wally himself felt completely fulfilled, it wasn't hard to imagine Joel might have been getting bored, complacent.

The object was to end up in a hot one-night stand—in either the marriage bed they'd shared for thirty years or a sleazy motel along the riverfront.

The idea had potential. And it could be fun, Wally conceded to himself, even while another side of him ached to simply ask Joel to turn the car around and go home. He was scared they were hurtling toward a line in the sand, a future that couldn't be changed once the machinery was set in motion.

He could lose Joel. And the thought brought a lump to his throat and hot tears to his eyes. He turned his head away, pretending to be absorbed in whatever could be glimpsed in the dark, dark night.

After a while, Wally forced himself to say, "Sure. It's gonna be fun. Shake things up a bit, right? Get out of our routine." And he knew he was saying the words only because he loved Joel so desperately and wanted him to be happy. Even if the cost had the potential of being great. Even if simply uttering these words of reassurance nauseated him.

They drove on in silence until they saw the flashing red and blue lights in the distance. As they drew closer, there was an ambulance, a fire truck, and a couple of police cars. Even closer, in the unforgiving glare of the emergency vehicle headlights, Wally noticed the black streaks on the road.

He swiveled his head as Joel drove by the accident. It looked like the pickup had swerved and crashed into the base of a big maple. It wasn't surprising, given the number of animals living in the woods that made a habit of darting out into the road, especially deer.

He looked for signs of life as they passed.

"Gee," Wally said. "I sure hope no one's seriously hurt."

"Or dead." Joel nodded.

Wally turned back around in his seat as they continued on, the night and its prospects spread out before them.

Anything could happen.

Chapter Six

Independence Day

Winslow Birkel sunk into the driver's seat of his beat-up Nissan Versa. At the little riverfront park, he marked the slow progress of a barge on the river, cutting through the dark water. Its lights, reflected on the water's shifting black surface, for no reason Winslow could figure out, were the very picture of loneliness, something Winslow could identify with.

His ribs still hurt, especially when he did something as outrageous as daring to take a deep breath. The bruise forming on his lower back, above where he imagined his kidneys, ached. In his mind's eye, Winslow saw the red marks, in the shape of fists, darkening to purple, a malevolent blooming.

Yet still, even with the bursts of nauseating pain, what hurt the most wasn't physical.

An hour ago, he'd fled the house he occupied—he'd never call it a home because home meant warmth, security, stability, and most of all, safety. He'd dashed out, looking over his shoulder at the menacing, broad-shouldered figure standing in the open front doorway of their house, fists clenched. Chad Loveless, his partner (he'd never call him his beloved, or lover, or even friend—not ever again), glared at him. This, Winslow knew from past experience and not because he could see Chad's eyes in the dimming light.

What had it been this time? Oh yeah, he'd broken Chad's favorite coffee mug, the one with a German Shepherd cartoon figure on a black background, as he was washing dishes. The mug had been slippery in his sudsy hands, and it had slipped. Winslow had gasped as it shattered on the linoleum kitchen floor, the dread and terror, way out of proportion, rose up immediately.

And so did Chad. He hurried into the kitchen from his recliner in the front room and forced Winslow to the floor by the back of his neck.

The most menacing thing about this man Winslow had thrown his lot in with (love no longer entered the equation) was—and this would be surprising to an outsider—his smile. The smile never wavered, not when Chad was berating him for some real or imagined fault, nor when a fist connected with a soft spot on Winslow's body—rarely his face—it was their little secret, hidden by the baggy jeans and sweatshirts Winslow now favored.

He'd smile and smile and smile, as though what he was delivering was not pain and casual cruelty, but joy.

Joy had not had a place in their house for such a long time. Winslow didn't know if he'd recognize the emotion if it turned up at the front door, wearing a ribbon.

Winslow got out of the car, wincing and groaning a bit from the simple movement, and the smell of fish from the river immediately rose up. Rather than finding it unpleasant, Winslow took comfort. The scent made him think of summer days when he was a little boy, when his parents would get together with their friends and they would go water-skiing on the Ohio River and then end up on Babb's Island, the tiny, tree-covered strip of land in the middle of the Ohio, to sit around long picnic tables, eating hamburgers and hot dogs and drinking beer. One of Winslow's earliest memories was going around one of those picnic tables, when the adults had vacated it to swim or fish for bluegill, and draining all the empty mugs, cans, and bottles of their beer.

He'd been so sick that night he'd never drunk again—not beer, not whiskey, not vodka, not wine.

One of the things he'd loved about Chad when they first met was how *he* never touched a drop of alcohol either. Winslow had seen too many of his young gay pals and playmates chasing oblivion with alcohol and worse. Relationships with them, not surprisingly, never worked out. Chasing a buzz was always easier for most than chasing stability and romance.

Chad had been different. Winslow had entered delightfully and all too fast into a relationship with him just last winter, right after the holidays. That they'd only been together for a few months always surprised Winslow because right now, it was a life sentence, a hell he was unable to escape.

Unable or unwilling? A voice rose up inside to question him.

Another voice, maybe his mom's, came up to chastise him. *Marry in haste. Repent at leisure.*

Oh, shut up, Mom. I'm not married to him, not technically anyway. Don't I have enough on my plate without you hectoring me? Haven't I been punished enough?

Winslow wandered down the water's edge. He found a boulder on the downward slope to the river and he sat. For a long time, he didn't allow himself to think. He was grateful for the ability, this once, to simply let himself *be*, to let his mind rest, to not worry, worry, worry about the future, or the regrets of his past. For now, there was only this humid darkness, the leaves whispering in the trees overhead, and the music of the crickets and cicadas.

Fireflies danced nearby, flashing golden for a moment, then darkening.

All at once, he remembered a summer night much like this one. The memory sprung from nowhere in particular because he wasn't thinking. But there it was—vivid, if incomplete.

His mother and he were being let out of a car at the corner of their street—at Mulberry and Ohio Avenue.

Winslow didn't remember the driver or where they'd been that night. But those details weren't important. He was only four or five years old at the time.

His mother was beautiful and he saw her so clearly in his mind's eye—a pair of shorts, a loose-fitting sleeveless floral blouse, her dark curls framing her face. She grinned. "I'll race you home."

And they were off, laughing, up the brick-paved street toward their green-shingled house on the corner.

Winslow also doesn't recall who won the race that night.

It didn't matter.

What *was* important: the moment he had with his mom, just him and her—alone. Winslow couldn't remember many times like that, where he got Mom all to himself. There was something young and carefree about her that night too. He had a glimpse of the girl she must have been before she married his father and became a mother to Winslow.

It was just the two of them and that's what brought the memory to the surface.

Winslow wondered then about her marriage to his dad. She stayed with him until he passed of an early heart attack at age forty-five. Stayed with him even though he lived like a single man, out at the American Legion or the VFW almost every night of the week. Stayed with him even though their fights were legendary. His browbeating her—and worse—kept Winslow pinned to the surface of his twin bed on those nights, hurting for his mom while he feigned sleep. His father's rage was like a fire burning out of control.

She even stayed with him through the many times he hurt her physically—pushing her into the car so fast she hit her head on the doorframe, slapping her in the ears so she couldn't hear right for years afterward, knocking her down the stairs...

Winslow had begged her to leave him. His pleas never seemed to move her, although he did give her credit for never saying, "But I *love* him."

Was it simply inertia that kept her by his side?

Was it the fact that he was disarmingly handsome and, seeing his smile, one could never imagine the toxicity and cruelty that brewed beneath it?

Was it simply that she just didn't believe in herself? That she couldn't make it on her own?

Winslow never knew and now he wondered if he could ever possibly ask her.

How would she react if he told her he was following in her footsteps? Living with an abusive man who was charming and irresistible to the ignorant outside world? Would she be sympathetic, kissing his bruises and scrapes to make them all better? Would she advise *him* to leave?

How could she when she had never followed that advice?

Winslow stood, brushing the mossy dirt from his ass. A car raced by, its muffler loud, on River Road, behind him.

He had the choice of doing one of three things right now.

One, he could take a few steps, fewer than a dozen, down to the water's edge. He could wade in and let the dark current take him away, pull him under. His body would probably end up tangled in brush or a low-hanging branch at the river's edge, and people would shake their heads in mourning and disbelief, decrying the tragic loss of life for one so young. They'd put down the cause of death as a tragic accident, a slip and fall. The river's currents were strong and unforgiving.

But he would be free.

Two, he could get in the car and head on up the road to the Q, the only gay bar in the area, and one he hadn't been to in many months, since he'd met Chad. Perhaps in its seedy embrace, he'd find someone better than Chad (a low bar, so to speak, no pun intended). Or maybe, just maybe, he'd realize he could live again—find happiness, dance in more ways than one, and know that he didn't need a man beside him to be whole, to be happy.

It was a lesson his mother had never learned. And even though her separation from his dad wasn't through any choice of hers, the dysfunction of her marriage had left her scarred—vulnerable and mistrustful. She'd forever be alone, doing crosswords in the kitchen of her trailer, while an all-news cable channel blared forth from a tiny portable she'd bought at a yard sale.

Or, three, he could get back in the car and head in the opposite direction, back to the white-brick ranch he shared with Chad. He knew the script by heart now and tonight, anyway, wouldn't be so bad. The routine seldom varied—Chad would be remorseful, and he'd beg Winslow for forgiveness. His green eyes would well with tears, and he'd promise, for the thousandth time, to never do it again. And, for the thousandth time, Winslow could choose to believe him. They'd hug and kiss and fall into bed, making up.

It sounded idyllic, tempting.

But Winslow had fallen for his own lies and lack of self-respect one too many times.

He got into the car, started it up, and pulled out of the parking lot.

He paused only for a few seconds at the entrance to the road, wavering the tiniest of bits. Sometimes, the smallest steps were the biggest. Turn right? Turn left?

And then he pressed on the gas and headed in the direction of the Q.

Tonight, right now, things changed.

Chapter Seven

Your Cheatin' Heart

Chris Patterson was twenty-three years old and desperately in love for the first time. He'd met Sammy Duchene a little over eight months ago on the Adam4Adam hookup site, and after that first meeting, the course of his life irrevocably changed for the better.

Even though that first meeting was a simple hookup, two sets of hormones calling to each other late at night, that connection quickly morphed into so much more.

It bloomed into love.

That very night.

Sammy was still in the shower, and Chris listened to the sounds—the splash and spray of the hot water and Sammy's baritone, belting out a song Chris's mom used to listen to on an old record album of hers called *Tapestry*. The singer was someone named Carole King and she had a kind of husky, melodic voice that Chris associated with rainy days and his mom dancing around the house as she made a mess of dusting and vacuuming.

Sammy's voice, Chris thought, was actually more beautiful than Carole King's, which said a lot, he knew. But Sammy's deep voice had a paradoxically velvety and sandpapery quality that had the power to make Chris shiver, to actually get hard just from listening to him belt out "It's Too Late."

The voice seemed part of the steam escaping from under the bathroom door. It was warm, sensual, and made it hard for Chris to think of anything other than stripping down and heading into the bathroom to slip into the shower with Sammy.

He knew he wouldn't. They'd already had sex three times that day, which was one more than usual for them. Newlyweds, his best friend Andre called them.

"The magic will wear off soon enough," Andre had warned Chris more than once when they met up for their weekly breakfast at the Elite Diner across the river in Summitville. "Then you, or he, or the both of you will get restless. Before you know it, you'll be just like the rest of us queens, opening up your most perfect union to three-ways or more-ways...and you know you'll both be getting some strange on the side too. Face it, honey, gay men are pigs. Don't kid yourselves that you guys are any different." Andre snorted with laughter before slurping down the dregs of his coffee and eating his last slice of bacon.

"Never gonna happen," Chris said. "We're different than you two," Chris explained, the 'you two' referring to

Andre and his husband Bradley Jackson. The pair were known around the whole of the tristate as a couple who played together—and maybe a little less known as a couple who played apart. But they played a lot, Chris knew. He also knew that, increasingly, who they played with was often *not* the other.

Sad.

Whether he wanted to hear them or not, Chris would get all the gory details every week at their standing Monday morning breakfast get-together—what orgy Andre and Bradley went to that weekend; what supposedly straight husband joined them in bed the weekend before; or how they went for a boys' night out at the baths up in Pittsburgh.

What was the point of being in a relationship? Chris often wondered, but never dared ask. He didn't understand why. Was he afraid of putting Andre on the defensive? Or was he scared of looking like a prude?

So, Chris would smile and try to hide how *icky* these details made him feel. After all, he didn't want to sit in judgment of Andre, who'd been his best friend since they were in grade school.

Chris couldn't imagine a time would ever come when he and Sammy would even want to attempt such a thing. They were sufficient to each other. Hell, the rate they went at it, sometimes several times a day, how would one or the other of them even have the energy for another man?

Chris couldn't imagine it.

And then there was the fact that they were so much in love and had been since that very first night together, when Sammy came over and stayed and stayed, gradually moving his stuff in a piece at a time until one day they woke up, laughed, and realized they were living together.

Chris didn't believe a more perfect arrangement existed, or could exist. When he thought of his Sammy, he thought of the song his mom used to sing to him as a lullaby, "I Only Have Eyes for You."

Why would anyone else turn his head when he had the most ideal mate, only a few feet away, his fine, dark skin lathered up with suds and hot water sluicing off it?

Damn.

Chris rose from the chair. The hell with the fact that they were going out to the Q soon. The hell with the fact they'd already had sex three times that day.

He was joining Sammy in the shower.

It was all that mattered right now.

He quietly opened the bathroom door. Steam hissed. Chris grinned—he wanted his appearance in the steam and falling water to be a surprise. Hell, maybe they wouldn't even make it out tonight. And that would be just fine by Chris.

One by one, he dropped his clothes to the ancient black-and-white tile floor, impressed at his own ability to remain so silent while struggling out of the sweats and T-shirt. He was aided and abetted by the song Sammy's Bluetooth player had just shifted to, Lady Gaga's "Bad Romance."

Oh, honey, this is a good *romance. The best one ever. Where have you been all my life?* Naked, Chris stood smiling.

He took a moment to savor his happiness and good fortune, and then tiptoed across the bathroom to the vanity sink, where Sammy's Bluetooth speaker was paired with his iPhone, which lay in front of it.

And, just like that, with a single glance, the scales fell from Chris's eyes.

The blood in his heart and flowing through his veins turned to ice. He swallowed a gasp, because now, he *really* didn't want Sammy to know he was in the bathroom. His erection, a second ago, pointing proudly up at the water-stained ceiling, rapidly deflated, demoralized.

It all happened because he simply happened to look down at Sammy's phone. He wasn't being nosy or suspicious—he was neither of those things—but because he simply wanted to see if he could change to a different Lady Gaga song, "You and I," instead of "Bad Romance." He thought "You and I" would be a sweet backdrop to what he was certain would transpire in the shower.

Now, it seemed "Bad Romance" was the right choice after all.

Don't mess with the universe.

He crept quietly, and backwards, from the bathroom, wishing he could unsee what he saw on Sammy's iPhone screen.

Cum over again? You really rocked my world on Tuesday night. Need you inside me again.

Chris grabbed his clothes and shut the bathroom door with the utmost caution, pulling it close against the frame to ensure there wasn't even the slightest click. He took a deep breath and let it out in a sigh. He felt sick and slid to the floor, hoping his gut would settle and the bile burning his throat would subside.

Cum over again? You really rocked my world on Tuesday night. Need you inside me again.

Did I misinterpret the text? Chris shook his head, wishing that was the case. But he couldn't imagine a world where the text could mean anything other than what it said. *Where was he on Tuesday night, anyway?*

"Where you goin', hon?" Chris recalled asking him on Tuesday, just as the sky was painting itself with the lavender and gray of dusk. He'd assumed they were staying in, Netflixing and chilling. He'd even picked out a movie for them, *Rosemary's Baby*, one of Chris's favorites. He'd been shocked when Sammy had not only not seen it, but had never even heard of it. Chris was excited to introduce it to him, knowing he'd be mesmerized.

And now that he remembered it, he recalled what he hadn't noticed before—the way Sammy had quickly stuffed the phone into his pocket, the guilty(?) look of surprise on his face, the abashed smile. "A friend just called." He'd paused then and Chris mentally kicked himself for being so stupid. The pause was a stall tactic, a way to come up with a lie.

"Her grandma passed, and she's tempted to drink again."

Sammy had always been open with him about a past of drug abuse and drinking. But he reassured Chris early on that he'd been clean and sober for more than a year. "I don't need that shit anymore," he said. He attended twelve-step meetings faithfully over in Summitville at the Episcopal church's parish hall every Wednesday night. He read from Narcotics Anonymous's Book of Daily Meditations, *Just for Today*, every day.

"It's Brenda," he went on. "She was really close to her and she's terrified she might drink again; she's so torn up." Sammy had looked so concerned.

Chris shuddered—at how easily the lie came, at how manipulative it was, playing on Chris's sympathetic good nature. Now, he recognized a good cover. It indeed ensured he wouldn't ask more, even if he'd never heard of this Brenda before.

He watched Sammy go on Tuesday night with thoughts of what a catch he'd found—a kindhearted man. *Looks fade, but kindness persists.*

Cum over again? You really rocked my world on Tuesday night. Need you inside me again.

Now he knew the truth. He wasn't kindhearted at all, but a liar and a cheat. Chris's stomach churned. He was afraid he was going to be sick.

In the bathroom, the shower handles squeaked and the water stopped running. The rattle of the glass shower door opening meant Sammy was out, that he would now see his text. "I'll be ready in a few," Sammy called out.

I can't stay here. Chris grimaced as nausea grew. He felt trapped, claustrophobic in the one-bedroom apartment.

He hurried into their bedroom and dressed quickly in a pair of black denim cutoffs and an old Pittsburgh Pirates tank top. He stuffed his keys, wallet, and phone into pockets. At the front door, he slid into the pair of flip-flops he kept there.

Behind him, the bathroom door's familiar creak urged him to hurry.

It spurred him on. He was out the door and running toward his little Mazda hatchback.

Where the hell do I go now? Where can I turn?

It didn't matter. He simply needed to go. Chris got in the car, started it up, and backed down the driveway. As he was waiting for a pickup truck to pass, he looked up to see Sammy open the front door, one of their white towels wrapped around his waist. Even from this distance, he could see the confused look on his face. The angle of his head asked, "What are you doing?"

And there was a moment when Chris hedged. *Maybe I shouldn't go after all. Maybe there's a reasonable explanation. He loves me, only me, after all.*

Cum over again? You really rocked my world on Tuesday night. Need you inside me again.

Chris pushed down hard on the accelerator, sending up a spray of gravel as he got onto the road in front of their house. He headed off, not looking back. He angrily wiped the tears away from the corners of his eyes.

*

Sammy stared at the retreating car, eyebrows furrowed together in confusion. He had one hand raised, as though that would cause the car to stop...or go in reverse. It was unlike Chris to up and leave like that without a word. Maybe he needed something at the Walmart across the river to finish getting ready for their night out? Sammy shook his head and went back inside, closing the door behind him.

No.

There was an uneasy feeling in his gut. He didn't know why. He didn't know what. But *something* was out of kilter. Although the running off to a store for something Chris had forgotten *was* plausible, it was highly unlikely. If that was the case, why wouldn't Chris simply open the bathroom door and let him know what he was doing? That's what his Chris would have done in the past.

Plus, there was the way he paused and then practically spun out of their little gravel driveway, as though he'd really stomped down on the accelerator.

Sammy went back into the bathroom, where he'd left his phone on the counter. He'd shoot Chris a text to ask what was up. As much as he racked his brain, he could think of no reason for Chris to be angry at him. The whole day, they seemed just as Sammy thought of them—a blissful young couple still in their honeymoon phase and loving every minute of it.

Nothing had changed. So why would Chris storm out? It made no sense.

But then it didn't make any sense that he wouldn't have simply said where he was going and when he'd be back. His sudden departure was so out of character. Sammy picked up his phone, shaking his head. He couldn't think of a single time since they'd been together when Chris had done such a thing.

He pressed his thumb on the phone button without looking at the screen. When the home screen came up, he saw he had a text message.

He opened the message and gasped.

> *Cum over again? You really rocked my world on Tuesday night. Need you inside me again.*

"Oh no, you didn't," he said aloud. "Oh, fuck no!"

Sammy stared down at the text, squinting, hoping against hope his eyes had deceived him. "Why on earth?"

He almost deleted the message because, even though it was totally irrational, he felt a stomach-churning wave of guilt as he glared at the text, as though he were somehow responsible. Who would have sent him such a message? He hadn't hooked up with anyone since before he'd met Chris, and he certainly hadn't been "inside" anyone other than Chris on Tuesday.

"What the actual *fuck*?"

He clicked out of the message and sent one to Chris:

Where are you? I must have missed hearing you say you were stepping out. Get back to me. Worried.

He hung up the towel and moved into the bedroom. He got dressed with trembling hands, not in the clothes he'd laid out for their evening out, but in a pair of flannel boxers and an old green T-shirt with the sleeves cut off. He kept an ear cocked for the ring of his phone or at least the tone that indicated he had a text.

Nothing.

He went into the living room where he plopped down on the couch.

He opened the text again. To the screen, he whispered, "Who the fuck are you, man? This is not cool."

Chris must have seen the message pop up while I was in the shower. He didn't know how he could, but he must have drawn the wrong conclusion. *Doesn't he trust me? Shit, we get busy so often I don't have the stamina to go after other guys. Can't he figure that out?*

Still, if the tables were turned, Sammy wondered how *he* would react. The fact was they hadn't been in their relationship long. And that message left little room for misinterpretation. No room, actually.

Sadly, Sammy knew he himself would be suspicious. The difference would be he'd brandish the phone in Chris's face and ask him what the fuck was going on. He'd be jealous and enraged. After all, his world would have been tilted upside down. But he wouldn't *not* confront Chris. It would kill him not to. He'd need to know, right now.

And that was one thing he knew about Chris, even though they were still a relatively new couple—Chris was nonconfrontational—to the extreme. He'd go to ridiculous lengths to avoid it. Sammy had watched him eat *pasta e fagioli*, something he didn't particularly care for, one time at Fiorello's Italian restaurant, just because he didn't want their waitress to feel bad that she'd brought him the wrong order. Chris had actually ordered linguine with clam sauce.

She'd brought the linguine to him after he was halfway through the *pasta e fagioli* and looked at him with confusion. She joked, "Um, that was for the lady over there."

Chris had lifted the bowl up to her, as though she could now deliver its half-eaten contents to the woman at the next table. Sammy, grinning, had put his hand on Chris's arm, forcing him to put the bowl back down.

It was just one of many instances now that Sammy thought about that revealed how scared Chris was of confrontation. He never complained. He withdrew.

Which is exactly what Sammy figured he was doing tonight. He'd drawn a reasonable conclusion from the text and stormed out.

Sammy picked up his phone and shot Chris another text.

I think I know why you're mad. And I can explain.

That sounded like a cheater. He added:

I don't know who sent that message! Playing a sick joke, I guess. Or wrong number. It's no one in my contacts list. Come home, Chris. This is fucked up, but it's just a misunderstanding.

He hit Send.

And then he called the number from which the text originated.

But there was no answer. The call went straight to voice mail. "Hey, it's Andre. You know what to do and when to do it."

Sammy hung up without leaving a message. What would he say, anyway? *Andre?* Really? Why would he do that? *How did he even get my number?*

Sammy sat waiting in the silence for more than an hour. No text came from Chris.

Chapter Eight

Band of Gold

Once upon a time, they'd been young, and in the heat of their friendship, when one or the other of them had suffered a broken heart yet again, they'd promised the other if they got to age fifty and neither of them was married, they'd marry each other. They could be companions, there for the other during holidays, vacations, sad times, and glad times. They'd be family to each other.

And that was no small thing.

After all, they got along so well! They both loved old classic movies like *Citizen Kane, The Best Years of Our Lives, To Kill a Mockingbird, Sunset Boulevard, Casablanca, All About Eve, Lost Horizon, The Miracle Worker*, and so many others. They enjoyed the same kinds of foods—comfort dishes like meatloaf, baked mac and cheese, a good roast chicken, chili, and beef stew. And they both adored following up these culinary classics with old-fashioned desserts like chocolate pudding, peach cobbler, lemon meringue pie, or brownies.

They could spend whole Saturdays together, browsing for bargains at the mall, eating at Chili's or the Olive Garden, and ending up at the cheap theater to see a second-run movie they'd longed to see. They'd hike local trails and compare the pictures they took with their phones—lakes and rivers, rolling green hills, wildflowers, and once in a while, a rare bald eagle.

They loaned each other books, always leaning toward mysteries and thrillers—Ruth Rendell, Agatha Christie, Raymond Chandler, PD James, Patricia Highsmith, Elmore Leonard, Harlan Coben.

They'd grown up, side by side in Summitville, Ohio, seeing each other through the trials and tribulations of small town public school life, grades one through twelve. And when it came time to go to college, they both chose to commute to Youngstown State University. Donna became a librarian at Summitville's Carnegie Public Library. And Ralph went on to teach English—composition and literature—at a little rural high school, Beaver Local.

Anyone seeing the pair of them together would recognize them for what they were—an old married couple whose lives were so intertwined they couldn't be separated—the kind of couple where, if one died, the other would pass away within days because he or she would be so consumed by grief.

She, with her shock of close-cropped silver hair and dressed all in black, happily clung to his arm when they traveled about. He looked for all the world like an older Mr. Rogers, complete with khakis, button-down oxfords, and cardigan sweaters. And he had that same vibe—innocence and kindness radiated off him.

One would imagine their children and, of course, their grandchildren. Both of their faces were stamped with gentleness and decency. One could imagine grandkids celebrating the days Grandpa and Grandma arrived, most likely bearing gifts and food that would rot their little teeth.

One would see a couple whose devotion toward the other would inspire envy.

Appearances were not always what they seemed.

Donna knew she loved other women as early as sixth grade, when she had a huge crush on the student teacher that year. Mrs. Mateer was a willowy redhead with a constellation of freckles scattered across her button nose. She took a special interest in Donna and even encouraged her to write more poetry after seeing some of the surprisingly advanced odes the young girl had penned.

Donna had cried, alone, at the end of the year, knowing she'd be moving on to junior high school and that, even if she wasn't, Mrs. Mateer would be returning to wherever she'd come from. Donna didn't know where, but it wasn't here. Who knew where Mrs. Mateer would end up? And worse, who knew if she'd ever think of Donna again.

To this day, Donna didn't know where Mrs. Mateer was. But she still had an affinity for willowy redheads.

There *had* been women through the course of her six decades, of course.

In her freshman year of college, Donna had a secretive first romantic relationship with Ruby Jean Prescott, who was two years ahead of her and president of her sorority. They'd met in an introduction to creative writing class and had become fast friends and then lovers. It had all been blissful, under wraps, for almost a year, until one day Ruby Jean told Donna she couldn't do "this" anymore, that it wasn't natural.

The most cutting blow, though, was that Ruby Jean was getting married to some jerk from a neighboring fraternity, an accounting major who would whisk her away to the rarified air of Shaker Heights, Ohio. "It'll be okay," Ruby Jean had told her, blinking back tears. "This was great, sweetheart, but we both know it was a phase, just a little experiment. I'll change once I get married and settled." And she'd touched Donna's hand then. "You will too. You'll see—the right guy will come along and everything will change. For the better."

Donna had declined to be a bridesmaid and hadn't even attended the wedding.

She couldn't stand to watch. She'd never spoken to Ruby Jean again, although she'd heard through the grapevine that she'd borne six children and later, much later—divorced. She was now living in Palm Springs with a woman who had her own vegan catering business.

There were a few others through the years, but every woman she met was involved with a man—or a cat. And, in the end, there was never room for Donna in their hearts.

But Ralph, her best friend since grade school, had *always* been there to pick up the pieces of Donna's broken heart.

To Donna, Ralph had seemed asexual, a man who, surprisingly, showed no evidence of a sex drive. Unlike other men Donna had encountered, for whom sex was the be-all, end-all of their worlds, whether they were gay or straight—or somewhere in-between.

No, Ralph was Mr. Reliable, forever a backup plan when a social outing fell through. Or if she got sick, Ralph always came by first with a pot of his homemade chicken soup or a container of hot and sour from the Magic Wok.

It surprised, actually stunned, Donna when Ralph told her *he* was gay. Of course, she'd shared her orientation with him when they were teenagers, and he'd always been supportive, interested even, in her crushes and failed romances, but never in a prurient way. But Ralph? He didn't seem to have a sexual bone (pun intended) in his body. Donna thought of him like her grandma, in Altoona, whom she couldn't imagine ever having had sex, although if she didn't, how in the hell did Donna get here?

She just assumed Ralph was a loner type. Ace. Wasn't that the lingo these days? She'd always assumed he didn't think much of doing the nasty. Maybe he didn't go number two either—too indelicate. Or even if he did have a bowel movement, it would emerge, pristine, in a sealed plastic bag.

Ralph had suppressed his own desires for so long, he told her, they were now relegated to someplace deep inside him that he could no longer access. "I like to look," he explained. "I really *love* to look. Dark hair, dark eyes, olive complexions. Give me a guy with a baseball cap, a dark beard, and driving a pickup truck and just a glimpse as he drives by is enough to set my heart to racing and, also, to satisfy me."

He told her, once he'd come out to her, that there was no one in the world for him. He was in his sixties now and was okay with not having some passionate love. "Leave it for the young folks," he'd say.

What he wasn't okay with, though, was being alone.

And so, he and Donna had tied the knot a couple of years ago in a simple and quick ceremony. They'd gone to the county courthouse—she flaunting tradition in a black sheath with lots of sterling silver jewelry, a black fedora perched on her head and he in a navy blue suit and red and white rep-striped tie—and made their vows. She'd even shed a tear when she gazed into his shining eyes. And despite her passion for all things curvy and feminine, she had a sudden thought as he slipped the simple white gold band on her hand—*I love this man.*

Both expected to be a pair until death did them part, just as they promised.

But Donna, in the darkest recesses of her mind, wondered about her promise, if not Ralph's.

If there was one thing she'd learned in her six decades, it was that nothing remained the same in this life. Nothing. And everything we had was on loan—for however long.

Tonight, they'd head out to the Q, have a few cosmos, watch the kids dance and flirt and then, around ten o'clock, when the Q's dance floor was just beginning to really heat up, they'd head home in the Buick they owned jointly.

Home, they'd share a cup of Earl Grey tea, milky with lots of sugar as they both liked it, and then they'd head off to their separate bedrooms.

Part Two

Get the Party Started

Chapter Nine

Papa, Don't Preach

As always, Nels headed straight for the bar when he passed through the curtained doorway into the Q. The bar was his favorite place to hang, not so much because it was from where liquor was dispensed—Nels had never been a big drinker, even in his youth—but because he loved the look of the old, curving, massive hunk of wood. He imagined it had been crafted from oak or maybe even mahogany.

Someone had once told him, long ago, that the bar had been carted in from a different nightspot down the river in Marietta. The story went that it was saved from demolition of what had once been a speakeasy during Prohibition. It was certainly grander than the humble environment it now stood in. Its solidity, the patina of its aged and dark wood, and the feeling it gave Nels of having been around forever were all things he adored. The bar was strong, sleek, sexy even, a solid reminder of bygone times. He imagined gangster types gathered around it in dark suits, fedoras shading dark eyes.

He never quite got the story of what had gone on with the bar during the years between Prohibition and when the Q was opened, back in the '70s. Whatever its full past was, Nels could always rely on the fact that the bar was a survivor with stories to tell.

It wasn't going anywhere soon.

He pulled out one of the chrome stools, its top covered in deep-red vinyl, and sat.

Mary Louise came right over, smiling as she dried a beer mug.

"Ah, a familiar and welcome face!" Nels cried out, smiling himself. There was something in Mary Louise's disposition that made him believe she was always in a good mood and everything was right in her world. She never tried to hide who she was—and the one word that fit her, not unkindly at all, was big—big nose, big earrings and at least now at the start of the night, big makeup, artfully applied. Her clothes were tight, but flattering. One of the things Nels admired about her appearance was that it reminded him of Dolly Parton once claiming it took a lot of money to look as cheap as she did. Mary Louise probably subscribed to the same philosophy. Although her gray hair had a prominent purple streak, her eyelids aqua, her lips bloodred, and her mascara thick, she always looked beautiful and well put together. And she never seemed to glory in her appearance.

She was just Mary Louise.

Nels assumed she had no life outside the Q. If he was honest, he might realize he thought of her as always there behind the bar, a glass in hand, coming to life only when the bar opened for an evening's business.

Sometime, I should ask her what she does for fun.

"Hey, handsome!" she cried. "What are you having tonight?"

"I'll have a Vesper martini," Nels replied, naming James Bond's favorite cocktail.

Surprisingly, Mary Louise seemed to know that the Vesper was a combination of gin, vodka, and Lillet, the French aperitif white wine, because she said, "Shit. We're all out of Lillet. I'll put an order in. The boss will say no, though, to such fancy stuff. I can guarantee that."

"I was just fucking with you, Mary Louise."

Her eyes got big. "No!" She chuckled. "Rolling Rock?"

"Sounds good." He'd been drinking Rolling Rock since before it was cool, a hipster beer. He didn't know what possessed him but he added, "And let's make things interesting. Back that up with a shot of Jack."

"You got it." Mary Louise turned to the rows of bottles lined up in front of the big gilded mirror behind her.

When she set down his drinks before him, she eyed the bouncer, Billy, and then returned her gaze to Nels.

"Don't say anything, but it looks like there was an accident out on Plank Road. Pickup truck. Not sure who was involved yet, but we're worried it might have been someone on their way here." Plank Road dead-ended at its intersection with Route 61, where the Q sat, so it was a logical conclusion.

Nels took a sip of his beer. "No idea of who might have been in it?"

"We don't know yet, just that it was a gray pickup."

So many folks around here own pickups. It could be almost anyone. "Well, I hope they're okay."

"Me too. I tend to worry."

Nels downed his shot. "I didn't know that."

Mary Louise snorted. "They don't call me Mother Hen for nothing." She called over to Billy to start the playlist for the evening's music. It had been many years since the Q had seen live entertainment that wasn't tied in with a drag queen's performance. Now, they simply relied on dance music playlists from Spotify blasting out of a halfway decent Bose sound system. It was good enough to get people up and moving, especially when a line dance came up in the rotation.

In moments, the Pointer Sisters were singing, "I'm So Excited." The volume, for now, was relatively low, because Nels was one of the first to arrive.

Nels quickly downed the shot and then sipped his beer, watching Mary Louise continue her prep work—slicing lemons and limes, making sure there was plenty of ice, and wiping down the taps. She grabbed the remote and turned the TV above the bar on to reveal an old rerun of *Three's Company*. She scanned channels for something suitable for background video. She settled on what looked like Turner Classic movies. Bette Davis appeared on the screen and Nels recognized the movie, *Stella Dallas,* because he'd just watched it last week. The film was just beginning. Mary Louise set the remote control on a shelf under the bar.

"Good thing we can't hear that. I'd be a blubbering mess before it's over."

"You and me both, kid."

He didn't turn as the door opened and closed, opened and closed. There was the music of laughter and conversation, animated because people were *out*, in more ways than one.

Nels sometimes thought he should be like Theresa Dunn, the sad, promiscuous schoolteacher from one of his favorite movies from the '70s, *Looking for Mr. Goodbar*. He could see himself bringing a book to the bar to read while he sipped his beer and waited for someone who looked like Richard Gere to arrive and sweep him away. Only, in his version, Gere wouldn't be a sexually confused homicidal maniac, of course. He'd be as handsome as Gere, but instead of stabbing him to death, he'd make him breakfast in bed.

"Well, my stars, if it isn't Nelson DiCarlo, in the flesh!" A woman's voice came from behind him. The voice had a scarred, yet velvety quality that Nelson thought had to have come from way too many cigarettes. "I thought you were dead!" A sputtering laugh followed this last pronouncement.

He turned to find a woman about his own age hovering behind him. Ironically enough, she put him in mind of Diane Keaton as she looked today, with a mane of curly gray hair framing her face. She wore wire-rim round glasses and was clad in a tunic top and yoga pants, unusual for these parts. She appeared almost gaunt. The only relief from all the black was a large sterling silver pendant in the shape of a stylized owl.

And when she smiled, revealing the gap between her two front teeth, Nels at last remembered who she was, her name coming to his lips simultaneously with the recognition.

"As I live and breathe! If it isn't Miss Cathy Corak!"

"That's Ms. to you." She grinned and gestured at the stool next to Nels. "Taken?"

"Only by you. Have a seat."

She slung a huge black leather bag onto the bar and settled in, grinning at him all the while, as though this were a planned and long-anticipated reunion. She raised a hand to get Mary Louise's attention, and Nels gently grabbed her hand, surprisingly soft, and lowered it to the bar.

"I'm getting your first drink." He called Mary Louise over. "What are you having?"

Cathy looked at Mary Louise and said, "Gimme a Tom Collins, sweetie. He's the only man who's never disappointed me." She looked over at Nels. "Since you, anyway."

Nels chuckled and Mary Louise turned to make the drink.

More and more people filled in and the bar, dank and dark, began to warm, to feel like a party. The colored lights in the ceiling came on, casting rays of red, blue, yellow. The disco ball spun, shattering the colors and dispersing them.

"Sweet Dreams (Are Made of This)" began to play.

"My God, Cathy, how long has it been?" Nels racked his brain, trying to recall the last time he'd seen her. They'd been kids, mere kids.

They'd actually dated in high school, back when Nelson tried valiantly and desperately to fit in, to be one of the 'normal' boys. It had been a short-lived love affair, if love was the right word, lasting only long enough for Nels to lose his virginity to their class's sure thing. A teacher had once told Nels, after he'd broken up with Cathy, "If that girl showed everything that had been stuck into her, she'd look like a porcupine."

Nels had lost respect for that unkind teacher on the spot. She may have taught him a few lessons about the novel, *Sister Carrie*, but the most important one she taught him was that one simply doesn't talk about other people that way, especially when one is both clueless and in a position of power.

He'd never lost respect for Cathy, who disappeared back into the crowd of teens Nels was never a part of—the ones who got high at the bus stop before school, drank, and smoked on the patio outside the cafeteria. The ones most of his teachers thought of as beyond saving.

He now thought he didn't remember her being around at all senior year—no presence at the prom or graduation. It was like she vanished. It was more likely she'd moved away. Nels had paid her departure little mind back then.

And now, he felt an odd excitement at seeing her again, this woman to whom he'd lost his virginity and the only woman with whom he'd ever been intimate. He flashed on an erotic memory (or at least one that had him passing the straight boy test). A dark winter night, a few weeks before Christmas. He and Cathy had gone out to hang at the mall in Beaver, Pennsylvania, sharing an Orange Julius and browsing at Waldenbooks, Gimbels, and Chess King before she brought him home in her mom's car. They'd stopped in the parking lot of an elementary school to make out, and almost before Nels knew what was happening, Cathy's pants were off, his were around his ankles, and she'd lowered herself onto him. If there were five thrusts, Nels would have been surprised—the sex must have lasted all of thirty seconds.

Still, it was kind of sweet in its own way. Dirty and innocent all at the same time.

"Oh God, Nels, it's been so many years, decades. I left town the spring after you and I dated for that brief time. I went to live with my aunt down in Martin's Ferry and ended up, after staying with her for a while, heading out to California." She closed her eyes and Nels noticed then how old she looked, the crepe-like skin of her neck, the lines around her eyes and the thin vertical ones above her lips. She looked tired—and closer to seventy than sixty.

"No wonder I don't remember seeing you around senior year."

"Just now noticing?" She guffawed and shook her head. Mary Louise placed her drink before her and she took a big swallow. "Cheers!" she raised her glass and Nels clicked his green bottle against it.

Her question caused a flush of heat to rise to Nels's cheeks. He really *had* forgotten her in the flurry of senior year. And honestly, until tonight, he could count on one hand the number of times over the years he'd thought of her, which was strange when you considered it, because female or no, she was his *first*.

"California? Wow. Movie star?" Nels wished he could withdraw the question. It seemed stupid and maybe a bit insensitive.

Cathy took another sip of her drink and set it down. She closed her eyes for a moment as if she was in pain. "Uh, no. Waitress? Sales clerk? Yes? Drug addict? Yup. Lady of the evening? Only when I couldn't make ends meet." She snorted and finished her drink. "Sweetie! Can I get another? And one more Rolling Rock for my friend here."

"Sure thing." Mary Louise removed Cathy's glass and Nels's bottle and busied herself with getting refills. In no time, she set them in front of Cathy and Nels.

"Thanks. You were kidding, right? About the drugs and the prostitution?" *Please say yes. I hate to think of someone I knew, even briefly, having to stoop so low. I hate to think of someone I cared about, even years ago and for a short time, to be so lacking in love for herself that she'd allow herself to be exploited and numbed by people and things that would scar her irrevocably.*

Cathy's pale blue eyes met his. "I wish I was," she said softly. Her tone revealed a darkness he figured she was trying not very successfully to keep hidden. They were quiet for a while; then both swiveled their stools to face away from the bar. The dance floor was filling up. Blondie's old rap hit "Rapture" was playing, and it was drawing dancers up and out of their seats. Gone was the novelty of seeing same sex couples dancing together. Nels shrugged and without removing his gaze from the dancers asked, "So what brings you out to the Q tonight? You haven't switched teams, have you?"

She laughed and the mirth ended in a spasm of coughing Nels tried to ignore.

"Why not? I assume you did."

"Oh no, honey," Nels came back. "Baby, I was born this way." He ventured a quick glance at Cathy. "You were just a detour on the road to Gaytown."

Cathy reached down and squeezed his thigh and let go. "I know, sweetie. I knew back then, but I was a young girl, stupid enough to believe I could change a pretty boy's mind if I let him have me."

"It's funny, isn't it?"

"What?"

Nels shrugged. "We think we know everyone else's motives. We think we know *them*. Turns out, the older I get, the more I realize we don't know a damn thing."

"You can say that again." Cathy turned to the bar to rummage around in her purse. She pulled out a pack of Marlboro Reds. "Wanna step outside with me? I'm sure you don't smoke, but keep me company. How 'bout it?"

Nels called to Mary Louise. "Save our spaces, okay?"

"You got it."

Cathy grabbed her bag off the bar and he followed her out into the darkness. They wandered a few yards away from the parking lot, down toward the line where a small rim of grass met a forest. The air was warm and the crickets chirped. A pale sliver of moon, partially obscured by a few strands of gauzy cloud, was their illumination. Distantly, the bass of the dance music came to them.

Nels watched as Cathy lit up and drew the smoke in. Her exhale traveled upward until it was snatched away by the breeze.

Gravel crunched as more cars rolled into the parking lot. Distant laughter floated over.

"You didn't really answer me," Nels said at last.

"I know I didn't. I came out tonight hoping to find you."

Nels cocked his head. "Me? Really?" He couldn't imagine why a fling from his teen years would suddenly want to look him up. These days, didn't people use Facebook for that, anyway?

Cathy smoked and thought. "I'm back here for my ma's funeral."

"I'm sorry to hear that." Nels didn't understand the non-sequitur.

"Ah. Don't worry about it. We were never close. But I'm her only daughter and thought I should be here to send her off."

"All the way from California?" Nels asked because he couldn't think of anything else to say.

"Oh, I haven't lived in California for years. Too many bad memories." Cathy's face went dark, but she smiled through it. "I live down the river in Martin's Ferry. I own a little bed and breakfast and run a dog-walking business. It doesn't make me rich, but it does pay the bills and put food on the table. These days, that's enough."

"So... You came out to a gay bar to talk about careers?"

Cathy laughed. "You were always funny." She rolled her eyes and followed up with the tired quip, "But then looks aren't everything."

Nels chuckled to be polite. And then he was quiet, hoping that would encourage Cathy to speak, to say more. He realized, with a chill unrelated to the weather, that she'd come here to seek him out for something specific, but he couldn't imagine what.

She finished her first cigarette and lit the next off the butt of that one. She sighed and the exhalation floated out on blue-gray smoke that drifted up toward the moon. She regarded the glowing cherry for a moment and then locked eyes with Nels. "I called around. This is a small town. Hopewell. And apparently, you, Mr. DiCarlo, are here just about every Saturday night. I wanted to see you, so here I am. No, I don't swing both ways, and these days, I don't swing at all." She lifted her cigarette for a moment. "These days, these are the nastiest vice this old gal has. And don't you dare try to take them away from me. I know they'll kill me one day." She paused to take a deep drag and blow the smoke toward the inky sky. "And that's okay."

"Why *did* you come to find me?"

"Don't you know?"

Nels felt yet another chill. Somewhere deep inside, he *did* know or at least had an idea of a possibility but didn't want to acknowledge it. Just as he'd always been gay, it took him until he was well into adulthood to acknowledge it.

"I thought it was time you knew. My mom passing made me realize none of us has all the time in the world. Parents' deaths tend to do shit like that to us."

"Knew what?"

"Nelson. We have a kid. A boy."

It felt as though every ounce of air he had inside rushed out. Even though it was melodramatic, he clutched at his heart. "From that one time? It only lasted a few seconds."

"Nelson! A few seconds is all it takes. Shouldn't be that way, I know, but it's the truth and probably the reason so many of us are walking around today."

He thought of the unkind porcupine comment that one teacher had made regarding Cathy. "I apologize for asking and certainly mean no disrespect, but are you really sure he's mine?"

Cathy laughed. "No worries. And I didn't expect you *not* to ask. I know everyone thought I was the class pump, the easy lay, Rosie Roundheels, whatever. The truth was that we were both virgins that night in the front seat of my mom's Valiant."

Nels's mouth fell open in surprise.

She laughed at his reaction. "Mean girls and weak boys wanting to make themselves bigger than they are started the rumors somewhere around eighth grade. Unfortunately, they stuck. But the truth was, you were my first. And my only—for a long, long time." She shrugged. "And then, well, let's just say that all changed."

"That's why you left?"

"Yup. Funny how I went away to a place I swore I'd never return to, and now I've been living there for fifteen years or so, ever since I got my shit together and got sober."

"Sober? But—"

She cut him off. "I know what you're thinking. Yes, dear, I was having a cocktail or two. Honey, booze has never been a problem for me. I know AA and all the other twelve-steppers take an all or nothing approach, and I took it once, too, but that's bullshit. I repeat—booze has never been a problem. Coke was a problem. Sex was a problem. With those two things, enough was never enough." She shook her head. "But I didn't come here to talk about addiction or even getting clean. I just came because I was in town and thought I should take this time to at least let you know you have a kid! Congrats, Papa!"

Nels couldn't join her in her laughter. His face felt numb, his knees weak.

"What happened?"

"When I found out I was pregnant, my ma sent me to Martin's Ferry to stay with her sister to save our family from "embarrassment," as she put it. Kind of ridiculous because we were always white trash, anyway. No one would have been surprised that I got knocked up, although they might have been a little stunned at who the daddy was. Anyway, long story short, I was in confinement, as they say, with Aunt Jackie for the whole time. I gave birth, held him for a few minutes in the delivery room at the hospital, and I never saw him again." She blinked hard and looked away.

"You had a boy?" Elation and utter shock were running a race inside. He had no idea which would—or could—win.

Cathy nodded. When she turned to Nels, he could see the tears standing in her eyes. "Not a day goes by that I don't think of him, wonder where he is, how he turned out." She looked down at the ground.

"Couldn't you find him? I mean, I hear about people reuniting with their put-up-for-adoption kids all the time."

Cathy shook her head. "The records were sealed, as was the custom back when he was born. Besides, most of my life, I was such a mess that I didn't think I had the right. Nor did I want to intrude on his life."

Nels looked up at the few stars shining through the clouds. "Now you have me wondering about that boy." He shrugged. "I guess he'd be a man, now." In his mind's eye, Nels saw him—a handsome young man with Nels's dark hair and olive complexion. For some reason, his imagination made him a few inches taller than Nels. He also sported a beard. He was smiling and there was something of Nels's late mom in that smile—kindness, humor.

Cathy broke the silence that followed, "I'm sorry. I hope I didn't upset you. Mom dying just made me look at life different now. Plus, my own health isn't that great, probably because I was so rough on myself for so many years. Don't worry, it's nothing serious. But who knows how long any of us will be around? You asked if I tried to find him, and even though I haven't, you might want to give it a try."

Nels imagined the young man in his head moving toward him, in slow motion. He raised his arms to hug him. Nels shook his head.

"Are you okay?" Cathy asked.

"I don't know, Cathy, to be honest. This night will always now be a dividing line between knowing and not knowing. I always wanted a kid, but I knew it was never in the cards for me. It never occurred to me that, all along, there was some little guy out there with my—and your—DNA running through him. I don't know what I should do with this now."

Cathy moved closer and placed a hand on his shoulder, gave it a little squeeze. "It's a lot to take in, hon. Give yourself time. You don't have to do anything right this minute, tomorrow, next week. You don't have to do anything, period." She shrugged. "But I thought you should know, so you could make your own choice. And, Nels? I'm so, so sorry I never let you know. That kid was, and is, half yours. I should have let you in on things." Cathy blew out a big sigh. "But I just couldn't, you know? I was too wrapped up in my own mess, and if it ever did occur to me, I didn't know if you'd really want to know. After all, we were just two kids fumbling in the dark."

Nels thought a long time before coming back with "No. We were so much more than that. We were the conduit to a new life, Cathy. I believe that boy must have wanted to come into this world so bad that he used our few seconds of fumbling to find his way here."

"Ah, a spiritual man. I knew there was a reason I liked you."

"You don't even know me." Nels regretted the comment as soon as it left his lips. "I'm sorry. I shouldn't have said that."

"Why not? It's true." Cathy stubbed out her cigarette in the gravel. She hoisted her big bag up farther on her shoulder. "Now that I've completely shattered your peace, I'll be heading home." She eyed Nels. "I'm so very tired."

"Are you sure? Come back in. I'll buy you another Tom Collins." Nels was desperate to know more, but even he realized Cathy had no more to give.

"You're sweet." She rummaged around in her purse and pulled out her phone. "Gimme your number and I'll text you back so you have mine." She grinned. "Twenty-first century matchbooks, eh?"

Nels rattled off his number and watched as she input it.

She turned. The parking lot had quieted, and Nels figured everyone who was coming to the Q tonight was now already here. Did he really want to go back inside?

He felt he and Cathy were suddenly strangers—again.

"It was good to see you, Nels. You were always so handsome—and you still are. I won't insult you by saying that's a waste. I'll be here through Wednesday if you want to talk more, and I'm always just down the river too." She began to walk away and Nels noted the sag of her shoulders, the slow deliberation of her steps, as though walking pained her.

She turned and came back. Nels was surprised when she kissed him, very gently, on the lips. "Believe it or not, you're proof to me that there's good in this world."

She didn't wait for a reply. She simply walked away.

Nels wasn't sure what he would have said, anyway.

He stood for a long time in the darkness, not thinking, but letting the wind, cooling, caress his face and indulging himself with that mental image of his boy.

Then he turned and went back inside.

Chapter Ten

The Stranger Redux

Riccardo checked out his reflection one final time before heading off for his biological father's house. He looked okay and not wanting in any significant way. There was no threat in his open features and hoped the man whose DNA he carried within him felt the same.

He'd traveled all the way from New York to meet him. His desire wasn't fueled by anything more than a need to meet at least one of his blood ancestors, so that the child he had on the way might know a little bit about his own roots, his familial and ancestral story.

He glanced down at the Movado watch his parents had given him upon graduation from McGill University in Montreal and saw that it was almost nine p.m. He hoped it wouldn't be too late to pay an unannounced visit to the man his Ancestry.com test revealed as his biological father, a guy named Nelson DiCarlo.

Riccardo hoped, through this connection, he might also find his biological mother. None of the subsequent research he'd done after discovering DiCarlo was his father revealed any other links, a fact that saddened Riccardo. His wife, Maya, had told him to keep his expectations low, that his *true* family consisted of the people who'd so lovingly brought him up. And that was after she'd grudgingly given in, when originally she'd told him to simply let things be.

She was right about his *true* family of course. But he felt that the son on his way deserved to know his family of origin, especially since the grandparents Riccardo could have introduced him to were now gone. There were practical reasons, too, to know the people from whence one came—heredity, medical conditions, things like that.

"This is a fool's errand," Maya had told him before he headed out for the airport. "You're probably only going to stir up stuff that shouldn't be disturbed. This guy probably doesn't even want to see you—after all, your conception happened decades ago, and who knows under what circumstances? Has he ever once sought *you* out? Please, Ric, just stay home."

He couldn't, of course, listen to her, even if he did simply want to remain with her in the comfort of their Chelsea one-bedroom.

Fact was, he was terrified to undertake this mission. There were so many questions and so many bad results he could encounter.

What if his dad was a horrible person?

What if he wanted nothing to do with Riccardo?

What if he simply denied him?

Or, what if his biological father was sick, impaired, or even dead?

He didn't think this last idea was true, because he'd found—through a records service he'd paid for online—an address and other contact information for this Nelson DiCarlo. He'd wished for a social media link, so he could have a look at the man and perhaps see a little of what he might expect, but Nelson DiCarlo stayed off the radar, if not off the grid.

But an address didn't necessarily mean a person was mentally fit, healthy, or even alive. What if he found yet another parent connected to him was dead? He didn't know if he could bear that.

And what if he arrived at this address and found it the home of a large and happy family? How would it feel to discover a possible mother, stepsiblings? And would he feel he was upsetting the apple cart, changing the lives of these relatively innocent people with a simple knock on the door?

It was a chance he'd have to take.

Riccardo smoothed his white button-down shirt, gazing at himself in the mirror, and then checked to make sure he had his wallet and keys and set off.

*

The house was small.

Riccardo wasn't sure what he expected, but the white brick ranch was so, so unremarkable. It could generously be called midcentury modern. From the outside, Riccardo could guess the layout—one entered the living room/dining room combination through the front door. Beyond that was a kitchen, which he imagined would be yellow with Formica countertops and painted cabinets, Priscilla curtains at the window over the sink, which overlooked the backyard. Go the other way and there would be two bedrooms with a small bathroom in-between.

Enough musing.

He listened as the engine died down—he had pulled to the curb in front of the house—and told his imagination, always overactive, to calm the fuck down. No, Nelson DiCarlo didn't live in a mansion, nor a shack with no running water or electricity, nor a geodesic dome, nor an igloo, or a shotgun house, or something propped up on stilts near a body of water.

He lived in a very ordinary house.

The street could have been found anywhere in America. It was quiet this time of night, no traffic. Streetlights made pools of illumination all the way down to where it made a turn about a half mile away at the base of a big, hulking hill. All of the houses were similar in size, denoting a calm middle-class neighborhood. Wind rustled the leaves above his head and Riccardo mused that the sound was akin to applause. There were mailboxes at the end of each driveway, and each house had its own detached garage. The homes didn't look new, but they were all well-kept, with neatly manicured front lawns and mature trees, maples, oaks, creating a kind of canopy over the narrow two-lane road.

It was the kind of place Riccardo imagined the aliens landing in an episode of the *Twilight Zone*, or where the zombie apocalypse might begin. He smiled grimly—Pittsburgh was where the original zombie frightfest—*Night of the Living Dead*—had been filmed lo these many years ago.

Riccardo tapped the steering wheel a couple of times and took a few deep breaths. "You can't sit here all night," he said, glancing over at the neat ranch. Yellow lights from within gave off a warm, homey illumination. There was a big picture window in the front of the house, and Riccardo realized there was a couch pushed up beneath it because there was a dog reclining across its back, watching the street, or maybe watching him. "You came all this way. See it through." A part of him, deep down, prayed this Nelson person wasn't home. At least then, he could wait until tomorrow.

"Get out of the car."

He opened the door and stood in the street. Distantly, he heard the doggie in the window begin to bark. He looked at the house and saw the mutt had stood. As he neared the house, the dog began barking more frantically. It looked like a wiener dog with a bad perm. Its tail was a wagging blur.

Riccardo stepped up onto the concrete slab that constituted a front porch, opened the screen door, and knocked.

The dog disappeared from the window, and he could hear it going crazy inside, yipping and scratching at the door.

His wish that no one was home might just be coming true.

He knocked again and heard the dog panting and whining at the door.

Riccardo allowed for three more rounds of knocking but when there was no result, turned away, both dejected and relieved.

He let out a little gasp when he encountered an old woman standing behind him in the darkness. She reminded him immediately of the actor, Jessica Tandy, perhaps how she looked as a nursing home patient in the movie, *Fried Green Tomatoes*. She was even dressed in a worn black-and-white housedress and cardigan. A pair of slippers, fleece-lined, covered her feet.

"Nelson ain't home." She eyed him, her head cocked. "Gone out."

"Yeah, I see that."

"You're driving poor Homer nuts with your pounding."

"Is that his name?" Riccardo didn't think about how the knocking and barking could probably be heard several houses away in this quiet neighborhood. *Toto, we're not in Manhattan anymore.* "My apologies, ma'am. I didn't mean to disturb you." He edged by her. "I'll get out of your hair."

"No skin off my nose, mister." She followed him down the walk next to the gravel driveway, all the way to his rental car.

He unlocked the door and opened it.

"If you want to find Nelson, he's over at the Q. Goes just about every Saturday night."

"The Q?"

"A saloon, a nightclub I guess they call it."

And, just like that, Riccardo was back on track for coming face-to-face with dear old dad. "Where is it?"

"Just down the main road a piece. Ten minutes, maybe."

Riccardo didn't think he'd ever heard anyone, other than characters in books or movies, describe distance as "a piece." Nonetheless, the old woman happily gave him directions, if only to get rid of him.

Riccardo thanked her and got in the car. He watched the old woman tread slowly to the house next door, a two-story with green-stained shingles and white trim. He waited until she went inside and turned off her porch light.

He started up the car and glanced back at the house.

Homer was back on his perch, watching. And this time, Riccardo was certain the mutt was indeed watching him.

Chapter Eleven

Livin' on a Prayer

It was the dream, that damned dream, that had her driving through the darkness. Gracie really intended to stay home tonight and had acted on her promise to herself—a grownup at last.

But she'd dozed off reading *You Matter* on the bed, propped up by a mound of pillows. As soon as her eyes closed, the dream started. In it, she was dancing alone with Rose. She held her close as the two of them twirled slowly around a dance hall, lit by colored spots that blurred and morphed, changing from blue to red, to purple, to orange, yellow. It didn't matter—the only light for Gracie was the illumination shimmering out of Rose's wide-set blue eyes.

In the dream, Rose was her young self, maybe even on the night they met all those years ago. Her blonde hair, shoulder-length, curled around her face. Her color was high and even in the dimness of this dance hall, her cheeks gave off a rosy glow. Her smile, only and always for Gracie, was perfect. She looked like Reese Witherspoon, but really so much better, so much more genuine than the movie star. Rose's lack of self-awareness of her own beauty only made her more attractive.

Their bodies fit together perfectly as they spun and stepped around the floor. The darkness revealed silhouettes of people watching, but Gracie couldn't care less. Rose was in her arms and fit against her like the missing piece of a puzzle, and nothing else mattered.

Gracie woke with a start, almost as though she'd had a nightmare, even though the dream was, perhaps, the fulfillment of her most fervent wishes.

Pickles eyed her from her perch atop the pillow next to Gracie. In the cat's single eye, Gracie saw understanding, as though she knew exactly what fantasies her mistress's subconscious had cooked up.

A sense of longing rose within Gracie, familiar but yet unusual in its intensity, in its very want.

Why isn't it you lying on the pillow next to me, Rose? Why isn't it you?

Gracie turned and reached for the book on her nightstand and then dropped her hand. She was in no mood to read anymore. The book didn't even have the power to lull her back to sleep.

She sat up and switched on the little lamp on the nightstand. The room filled with warm illumination.

"I remember that young girl," Gracie said, maybe to herself, maybe to Pickles, maybe to no one at all.

In her mind's eye, Rose, on the night they met, came into view. Because it had been country western night at the Q, Rose had worn a faded denim miniskirt, a red-checked blouse tied off at the waist and revealing a tantalizing glimpse of smooth, tan belly, and cowboy boots, black and red. Gracie could see her by the silvery light of the full moon. They'd both just danced together to "Boot Scootin' Boogie," and Gracie had proposed they step outside to let the cool air dry their sweat.

Those moments in the moonlight had been magical and Gracie remembered how hard she'd been thinking, longing, and looking for a perfect moment to lean in and kiss this woman she'd just met and who, with a single dance and a single glance, had turned her world upside down. Even now, she could remember how fast her mind was working—when to ask Rose out, where to take her, how to delight her...

But just as she'd gotten the courage and was moving in for the kiss, Rose's friend Liz had emerged from the bar. "Hey Rose! You out here, sweets? They're playing our song!"

And just like that, the spell broke, snatched up by the wind. Now Gracie could swear she could see the failed moment, like a wisp of cloud, floating up toward the star-studded night sky.

The spell had been irreparable for decades, and in her lowest moments, Gracie tried to content herself with the certainty there was no getting it back.

"And why the hell not?" she asked Pickles.

If Pickles knew, she wasn't saying. Or maybe Pickles knew the simple truth that humans, in their warped self-awareness didn't realize—that it was *never* too late to reach for the brass ring.

Gracie sat up more fully, knowing that the idea of falling back to sleep was off the table for now. Something nameless—and relentless—pressed her to get up and dress, follow the script already laid out for this night.

And now, she found herself taking her foot off the gas a little to slow down.

Her gut was in her throat as she gaped at the flashing lights of emergency vehicles, at the twinkle of broken glass, like jewels scattered across the pock-marked asphalt.

"No!" she cried, guttural, as she veered to the side of the road and threw her car into park. "No," she said again, more softly, as she threw open the door.

The last *no* barely reached her lips as she stood, frozen for a moment, across the road. There was no doubt—that was Liz's F-150 smashed into the side of a big oak tree, steam still rising from its crumpled hood.

Breathing hard, she rushed across the road, the broken glass crunching underfoot and the smell of antifreeze rising on the night wind.

A police officer in uniform, a kid really, with a blond buzz cut and worried eyes, put up an arm to hold her back. "Please, ma'am, get back in your car."

Gracie stopped only a few feet away from the crashed truck. The silence got to her most. It crept inside and sent ice water up and down her spine. She wanted to scream. She wanted *them* to scream, because any sound, even one of terror, would be preferable to this deadly silence.

She leaned to see around the uniformed officer. Maybe she'd catch a glimpse of Rose or Liz in the front seat, bloody, maybe, and confused, for sure, but *alive*.

But the truck's cab was dark. It looked empty.

"Ma'am? I need you to get back in your car. Let the EMTs do their work."

Gracie wanted to slug him. "But these are my friends, my dearest and best friends. I was supposed to be with them!" She almost screamed the last part. And she almost wished she were with them.

He glanced at her and the sympathy in his eyes made her grateful. "I'm sorry. They're taking them to the hospital in Wheeling."

At the mention of the hospital, the ambulance's back doors slammed shut. Gracie watched, shaking, as it tore off down the road. There was no siren.

"Are they okay? Are they gonna be okay?"

The officer's face was blank—Gracie could read nothing from it. "Please! Are they?" She tapped his shoulder.

"I don't know!" he snapped. And then, as though he realized he was being too sharp, he softened his tone. "As I said, they're taking them to Wheeling."

"You really don't know anything else?" Gracie just knew he was keeping something from her, and she couldn't bear to think *what*.

He laid a hand on her shoulder and squeezed. "I really don't. If I did, I would tell you, even though I probably shouldn't. Okay?" He paused, maybe waiting for a reply. When he didn't get one, he went on, "My advice? Get in your car, calm yourself down, and then go to the hospital. They'll know more there, and maybe you can even see your friends."

"But it looks like a terrible crash!" Gracie wailed. She glanced over at the shattered windshield, the crumpled hood.

"I can't—" The officer began to say, but Gracie didn't wait for what empty comfort was about to sprout from between his lips. She dashed back across the road, narrowly missed by a black SUV. Its horn was a Doppler cry of alarm in the night, fading fast as the car headed onward.

She got back to her car and slid into the driver's seat. The engine was still running, lights on, but Gracie gave herself a moment, just a moment, to follow the officer's advice and to calm down. She whispered a petition to whatever god might be tuned into her own personal drama this awful night.

"Please, please let them be okay."

She shifted the car into gear, checked the road, and then stomped on the accelerator, praying also she'd find her way to the hospital in Wheeling without trouble.

She also promised this god that if she would just let Rose and Liz be okay, she'd finally confess her love for Rose.

"Just give me that chance!"

Chapter Twelve

Living the Lie

Wally sucked on the straw in his rum and Coke as though the cocktail was life-giving sustenance. It comforted him. He felt like a baby with its bottle.

He couldn't do it—play the game in which his husband Joel wanted him to participate. In the interest of spicing up their three-decade-old relationship, Joel's notion of pretending not to know one another so they could meet up for a one-night stand was a little too out there for staid Wally. Even though Joel assured him that all they'd do was *talk* with others, maybe even flirt a little, the objective was always, of course, of ending up in spousal arms at the end of the evening. It was just that Wally feared that accepting this new normal might set a new line in the sand, one that was permissive.

Wally shook his head, gazing around the run-down bar, at the folks on the dance floor, oblivious to his presence. He'd never been here before. He'd never actually liked going out to the bars, even when he was young and relatively pretty. To him, they felt vaguely—or not so vaguely—predatory. He couldn't help it—there was always the sensation every man in the bar was simply looking just past Wally for something slightly better.

This whole evening felt strange, like something his mom would have read about in one of her *Redbook* magazines when he was a little boy, or maybe one of his dad's hidden *Hustlers*. He should have simply told Joel no, but he hoped to be accommodating. He didn't want to seem square or unwilling to be a little adventurous.

He slurped down another mouthful of the sweet drink, unable to avoid the truth—Wally actually *was* square; he *was* unadventurous. He'd been a CPA all his adult life, for cryin' out loud. He drove a Buick. He was Episcopalian, and although he hated what the GOP had become in recent years, he was conservative in political matters.

He would have been content to simply stay home tonight—a quiet comfort food meal, meatloaf and mashed potatoes maybe, a couple DVR episodes of *Grey's Anatomy* and early to bed seemed like perfection to Wally these days.

He couldn't quite grasp Joel's need to seek excitement outside their comfortable home, one they'd worked together over the years on making a sanctuary.

Maybe it was because, even in his own eyes, Wally *was* boring that he worried and went along with what he thought of as a cockamamie plan. He shrugged, finished his drink, and stood so he could amble over to the bar and get another one.

He looked for Joel, but the dancing crowd and the dim lighting made it impossible for him to find him. For a brief moment, his nerves became electrified, making Wally at first tingle in an unpleasant way and then feel a kind of nauseous dread, sour, in the pit of his stomach. He peered through the gloom once more, stopping just shy of the bar.

The faces in the crowd suddenly felt cold, devoid of emotion or even features. It was as though they were clay masks, imprinted with only the flimsiest signs of humanity. Wally had the sinking sensation this was because of his own belief that he was *not* one of them. He was too old, too tired, for this Saturday night nonsense. He had no desire to flirt with anyone other than Joel.

Yet, truth be told, it had been a long time since he'd flirted with Joel. Wally often joked he and Joel were an "old married couple," and by this, he didn't mean they were boring, but settled and comfortable. Those two things might not light up the night sky with fireworks but they were good things. Valuable. True.

He really didn't want to set up some alternate reality, even for a night, wherein he was single again. That state was not one of excitement for him. It never was. He didn't look back on his bachelorhood with fondness, quite the opposite. The bad dates, the drinking too much, the feeling he was never good enough, or that he was someone's closing-time-consolation prize all stayed alive, grim reminders, in his memory.

No, being single wasn't fun. It wasn't exciting.

It was empty.

All Wally had ever wanted was to ape his parents' own harmonious union. Other than his father going off every day to work for the railroad, Sam and Sarah were seldom apart. They did everything together, from lowly grocery store runs to cherished vacations. Rarely did more than a foot or two separate them. And the best thing? They never tired of one another. Wally couldn't remember a single argument or cross word between them. All he could recall was the sight of the two of them in the front seat of the car, pulling into the driveway. Or his mom stirring something on the stove and his dad swooping in for a taste with the big wooden spoon always on the rest in the middle of their gas range. He'd earn a smack on the arm for that and then, maybe, a peck on the lips. He remembered them on the couch in their living room, his father's arm draped loosely over his mother's shoulders as they watched yet another movie on TV or maybe an episode of *Kojak*.

Who loves ya, baby?

And maybe their relationship was rare, but it was true. The real thing.

And it had been all Wally had ever wanted.

He thought he'd found it, so long ago, with Joel. He always believed Joel felt the same.

But we can never truly know what's in someone else's heart or head, can we? No matter how close we get, we're always essentially alone. We don't know and can't know what goes on inside someone else's head, no matter how much time we spend with them or how much we love them.

Wally could look back, even if he didn't like it, over their recent years together and detect signs of boredom in Joel. A faraway gaze, a furtive glance at a hot runner, shirtless, on the street as they drove to the Giant Eagle supermarket, the sudden desire to find interests that didn't include Wally—a gay men's book club, a bowling league on Friday nights, even a meditation group at the Carnegie public library near their house on Monday afternoons—all of these things might have indicated to Wally that Joel was growing weary of their admittedly boring and vanilla routines.

But, stay in a marriage long enough, Wally thought, and you can make denial a kind of permanent state. *Of course, my Joel doesn't have a roving eye. How could he when we're the perfect match? Of course, my Joel doesn't think about being anywhere but within the confines of our home when he's staring wistfully out the window like a caged bird.*

Wally hoped he hadn't come to the realization too late that Joel was indeed drowning in ennui.

Go along, go along, a voice in the back of his mind chimed. *Otherwise, you could lose him.*

But if going along means going against the very fiber of my being, where does that leave me?

Wally didn't wait for that voice in the back of his mind to respond. He stepped up to the bar, signaled the bartender and ordered another rum and Coke. As she started away, he called out, "Make that a double, okay?"

"You got it, handsome!" She called over her shoulder, smiling.

Wally decided, mainly because of the kindness he read on the bartender's face, to grab an open stool at the bar. He tried not to think too hard—or too cynically—that her smile, warmth, and probably insincere flattery, were only inducements for bigger tips.

When she set his new drink down in front of him, atop a red paper napkin, she asked, "How you doin' tonight?"

And Wally blurted out, "I seem to have lost my husband."

Her gaze roved over the crowd. "He's probably in the can."

"Yeah, you're right."

She put down a glass she was drying, surprised that she suddenly had a free moment. Or at least that's how it appeared to Wally.

She leaned against the bar, resting her elbows on the worn, dark wood surface. She looked Wally right in the eye and asked, "You worried about him?"

And Wally started to wave her away and say something along the lines of the catch phrase of the great Alfred E. Neuman, "What? Me worry?" But then his mouth opened and the whole plan, sordid, pathetic, brilliant, however one chose to view it, came tumbling out.

Mary Louise, as she told Wally her name was, snorted with laughter and then sympathized. "I wouldn't worry. How long have you two been together again?"

Wally told her.

"That's a long time! For one, you should be proud. That's an accomplishment. Hell, I bet on any given night half the people in this bar are here trying to find just what you have."

Wally nodded.

"And he's been upfront with you, right? Honest about it?"

"Yeah, I guess so."

Someone at the opposite end of the bar was trying to get her attention, waving a bill of indeterminate denomination around in the air. She smiled, held up a finger to tell him hold on a second, and then returned to Wally. She rolled her eyes. "I gotta get back to my customers. But if you're looking for advice, I'd say just go along. Let Joe have his fun."

Wally didn't correct her for using the wrong name.

Before heading off to serve her new customer, she told Wally, "Listen. You don't have to participate. Just sit right there. I'll keep your glass filled, and we can chat when I can. When Joe's ready to head home, he'll come get you." She walked away.

Wally watched her, then spun his stool around to face the dance floor and the rest of the bar.

Joel was nowhere in sight.

Wally felt sick. He followed Mary Louise's advice to stay right where he was, but not because he thought she was smart or compassionate. He stayed on the stool because he was afraid if he got up to look for Joel, he *would* find him.

And he was even more afraid he wouldn't like what he found.

Chapter Thirteen

Pour Me

Poor guy.

Mary Louise put Wally out of her mind for the moment and hurried to the young man at the end of the bar, with his currency held aloft. She got the message.

She didn't say it, but the guy who'd "lost his husband" had most likely lost him in more ways than one. The fact he couldn't find him was worrisome, but Mary Louise didn't want to add to Wally's anxiety. As Doris Day once sang, what would be, would be. Mary Louise could offer a kind word, maybe even a bit of sage counsel, but her powers pretty much ended there. She couldn't, much as she would like to, wipe away things like jealousy, fear, or even the gradual deterioration of a relationship. She had to constantly remind herself that in the end she was a bartender and not a therapist.

Back to work.

"What can I get you?" she asked the guy standing in front of her. Like Wally, she'd never seen him before. If she had, she would have remembered, because this guy was a looker, what she and her friends back in Chicago would have called a hunk or a hottie. Somewhere around six foot two, he had a nice lean build. Runner, maybe? Dark hair, flecked with the tiniest bit of silver, green eyes, five o'clock shadow. There was something cosmopolitan about him, a certain urban vibe Mary Louise had almost forgotten existed. She'd been away from Chicago too long. Anyway, she could tell from a glance, he wasn't from around here.

"Do you have Stella?" the guy asked.

"I don't know, I'll check." Mary Louise leaned back and, doing her best Marlon Brando/Stanley Kowalski impression, screamed, "Stella!" She held a hand to her ear as though expecting a reply, then turned back to the guy, who had the decency to chuckle at her lame wit.

"Not here, huh?" he asked.

"I'm afraid she's out. But, to console you, we have Bud, Bud Light, Miller, Miller Lite, Michelob, Pabst, Iron City, and even Rolling Rock, if any of those would whet your whistle."

The guy set down the ten-dollar bill he'd been holding up on the bar. "Rolling Rock would be great."

She turned to pull a bottle from the cooler below the bar. "You wanna glass?"

"That's okay."

She shoved the green bottle toward him, and he slid the ten toward her.

"I'll get your change."

"Keep it." He took a swig of beer. *God, he's cute.* "Got a minute?"

Mary Louise said, "Sure."

"I'm looking for a guy." The young man sat down on a stool.

"Honey, so is everyone else in this joint, including me." Her gaze wandered over to Billy Breedlove, standing by the door. He looked bored. He looked delicious.

He laughed and extended his hand. "Riccardo."

She shook it and told him her name. "Well, Riccardo. What kind of guy are you looking for? Tall? Short? Husky? Bear, maybe? Thin? Rich? Artsy? Notice I didn't say poor. I've been known to play matchmaker on occasion, and I do believe you're new here, so I'm happy to help you out."

For at least a minute, Riccardo appeared to be at a loss for words.

He's impressed with my wit. Yes, I'll go with that.

"Um, I'm gonna assume you're kidding. I'm not looking for a guy in that way." He grinned, revealing a pair of twin dimples on either side of his face. "At home, my wife and even the kid on the way, wouldn't be on board with that."

Mary Louise wondered, *What the hell are you doing here, then?*

"I'm looking for an older guy. Nelson DiCarlo? I was told he comes here pretty regularly on weekends."

Mary Louise's focus shifted from Riccardo in front of her to one of the little high-top tables across from the bar and against the wall. Nelson DiCarlo himself sat there, drinking innocently, unaware he was being paged, so to speak. Mary Louise wasn't certain what she should do. She'd known Nels for years and had had many a long conversation with him, especially on slower nights in the dead of winter when not as many people ventured out to the bar. He was a warm man, the heart of kindness, and always made Mary Louise smile when he came in (early) and left (early)—he'd always make sure to give Mary Louise a parting smile and wave, no matter how busy she was. He was generous, both in tips and in kindness. She'd often wondered why he was alone. He was smart, funny, good looking...

And then she looked back at Riccardo. And then at Nelson again. *No.*

But she couldn't help it—there *was* a resemblance.

She wasn't going to give anything away though. She wanted to find out more about *why* this Riccardo person was looking for Nels. Long-lost older brother? Or maybe Riccardo was out to serve him some papers? Mary Louise couldn't imagine the latter—Nels was so mild-mannered and quiet she couldn't conceive of a situation where the man would be having papers served on him. Still, she wanted to protect him, even if he was sitting only a few feet away from this young man who wanted to meet him.

But if he was a process server, how would that explain the resemblance?

She took care of a couple more customers, serving a whiskey and a beer, and a club soda with lime, and then returned to Riccardo.

"So, uh, why the interest in Nelson?"

She watched as the wheels turned in Riccardo's head. *Was he contemplating lying to her? Don't even think about it, kid. One thing this job has given me is an amazing bullshit detector.*

Riccardo took a sip of beer and came out with it. "He's my dad."

Those three words shocked. Mary Louise felt weak in the knees. She shivered as an icy chill raced through her. Finally, she ended up with a fluttering sensation in the pit of her stomach that traveled up and up until it emerged from her lips as laughter. She laughed long and hard, doubled over, until her gut ached, and she feared releasing a little pee.

"Okay. That was great, Riccardo." Mary Louise wiped a tear from the corner of her eye and regained control of her breathing. "So, seriously, what's the deal?" *You a bounty hunter, maybe? I'm more likely to believe that than the fact that Nels could be your dad.*

"That *is* the deal." Riccardo drank his beer and watched her. He had a poker face, hard to read.

Mary Louise leaned over the bar, so she could be closer. "Look, there's no way. I've known Nelson DiCarlo for years, and believe me, if the man had any kids, I'd know."

"What if he doesn't know?" Riccardo shot back. He gave her the short version of how one of those DNA testing kits had led him to his dad, one Mr. Nelson DiCarlo.

"Oh, are you sure? Those kits aren't 100 percent."

Riccardo shook his head. "I'm not wrong. I've backed up the research. So, are you telling me my biological father is gay?"

"I'm not telling you anything. That would be up to him." Mary Louise suddenly felt uncomfortable. She was torn. Should she let this kid know his father—if that *was* indeed the truth—was sitting just behind him as they spoke? There seemed something invasive about it, unfair. To Mary Louise, it would be akin to an ambush.

In the end, she decided she couldn't do it. She was loyal to her loyal customers. She refused to lie, though; that wasn't part of who she was. In the end, she just said, "I'll, uh, keep an eye out, okay?"

She didn't give Riccardo a chance to respond but walked away. She had a line of customers now, impatient for their booze.

She'd tell Nels about the kid when he arrived in front of her for his next drink. He could decide what he wanted to do about it.

That's fair, right?

It was about a half hour before Nels stepped up to the bar again. Mary Louise felt her heart began to race and her pulse to flutter when she spied him with his empty bottle. This was *not* just another Saturday night. It had the potential to be life changing.

She took the empty from him, trying to quell the trembling in her hands. She got a new Rolling Rock from the cooler beneath the bar. For this process, it wasn't necessary to speak. Mary Louise knew what Nels drank as well as she knew her own name. Besides, she wasn't sure words would come out if she opened her mouth.

He took the drink and put a five on the bar. "Keep the change, hon." He started to turn and Mary Louise realized she needed to make a fast decision. *I can just let this go, ya know? I have no reason to involve myself.*

She recognized her thinking as cowardice. Like it or not, she *was* involved now. As soon as Riccardo had confessed to her that he thought Nels was his dad, she was part of their story.

"Uh, Nels," she called.

He turned around.

She tittered, actually tittered. Her nerves! She shook her head. Nels stared at her oddly, half turned toward her, half turned toward his former seat, in danger of losing it as Wally honed in on it. "What?" he asked, a little annoyed.

"I have something I need to tell you." The words came out in a breathless rush. She was glad no one was waiting to be served at the moment.

He returned to the bar.

Mary Louise considered for a minute. This wasn't a conversation to have over the bar, with some guy in a T-shirt with the sleeves ripped off waiting for his Bud Lite. She got Billy's attention and asked him to come over and take her place. He did that for her when she needed a break, which was seldom. He poured too heavily, often miscalculated change, and rarely smiled, but he was all she had in a pinch.

And this was a pinch.

Once she had everything settled, she turned to Nels. "You wanna step outside with me? God, I need a breath of fresh air."

"Okay," Nels sounded, understandably, a little leery.

Mary Louise led him out to the parking lot and toward the line of trees behind the bar.

"Are you gonna rape me?" Nels asked.

"You wish." Mary Louise laughed.

They stood in silence for a few seconds, she shifting her weight restlessly from one foot to the other and he staring up at the star-studded night sky.

"So what's this about?" Nels finally asked. "In all the years I've been coming here, no one has ever asked me to step outside. And tonight, two people have." He laughed. "And just my luck—both women."

Mary Louise swallowed hard and then came out with it. "There's a young guy inside. Says his name is Riccardo?"

"Okay."

Mary Louise drew in a breath and then looked Nels in the eye. There was no easy way to put the truth—no softening the blow that she could see. "He claims he's your son." She expected him to do what she did when confronted with the story. But he didn't laugh. He simply stared at her, lips parted.

"Wait. What?"

She explained about the DNA test and how he'd traveled here to Hopewell to meet his biological father.

"How old is he?" Nels asked. Still, no laughter, which gave her a chill despite the warmth and humidity of the night air.

"He didn't say."

"Could he be, say, early middle age?" Nels leaned in.

"Yeah, I suppose so." She paused for a moment. She'd expected laughter, a denial, an accusation that she'd allowed a crazy person into the bar. "Wait a minute. You're not denying this is a possibility."

He eyed her. "Anything is possible," he said softly.

"*Anything*? Really? I thought you were a gold star fag?" Mary Louise was comfortable enough to know he wouldn't be offended by the "fag" and would understand her reference—gold star meant he'd never slept with a woman. She could have sworn he'd told her that at one point in their knowledge of each other.

"Pretty much. But not 100 percent. So, it *is* possible."

And, finally, Nels laughed and laughed, almost into hysteria territory.

Mary Louise knew he wasn't seeing any humor in this situation. She had a sudden flash of memory.

*

The woman behind the glass smiles at me, as though this were any other day, as though this were just the usual doctor's office and not Planned Parenthood. She hands me a clipboard and asks me to fill it out. I take it and she explains that I'll see a counselor and have a short exam. "The procedure itself will only take about fifteen minutes."

I shudder at the word procedure, as though this was something as routine as the dental cleaning I had last month.

Her eyes crinkle a bit as she smiles. The kindness in her face radiates outward. I'm grateful because I'm scared out of my mind. She reminds me a bit of my Aunt Eleanor, who's always been single and always a friend to me. I wish she was here right now if for nothing more than to hold my hand.

I feel sick. I want to run. My best friend, Kevin, waits in his little Datsun pickup truck in the parking lot out back. He's not the father, but he does care about me in a big brother sort of way. He wants to be sure I get home safely, whether it's required I have someone to accompany me or not.

"You sure you don't want me to come in with you?" he'd asked, his brown eyes regarding me with concern.

I shake my head. "I got to do this on my own."

"No eighteen-year-old should have to do something like this alone." His hand is on the door handle.

I reach out a hand to stop him. "Please, Kev. Just let me go do this. I'm not alone. You'll be right here when I come out. And then you can take me home, and we can watch an old movie together and have hot chocolate. My mom and dad won't be home for hours."

He sighs and I know he disagrees. I also understand he is familiar enough with my quirks to know that arguing with me is pointless.

"M.L. Smith?" A lovely woman wearing a bright emerald green dress that compliments her red hair and nearly matches her green eyes, stands in the doorway to call me back. She reminds me a little of Ann Margaret. "You can come on back, hon."

She must be the counselor. What kind of advice will she give to a young girl who was a virgin before being sweet-talked out of it at a fraternity party? Will she be able to erase all the bad? Will she be able to make her feel like less of a fool for believing someone loved her?

Sick to my stomach already, I get up and trudge on unsteady legs to follow her.

*

Nels had calmed a bit. He still breathed hard, but the tears that had fallen from his laughing/crying jag he'd wiped away. "Do you think he's for real?"

Mary Louise gnawed her lower lip, leaned in, and whispered, "He looks just like you."

Chapter Fourteen

The First Time Ever I Saw Your Face

It was getting on toward ten o'clock when Winslow Birkel got out of his car near the Q. The parking lot was packed so much that Winslow ended up having to grab a spot along the side of the road. It was Saturday night, after all. Winslow could feel as much as hear the vibration of the bass from the dance music playing inside. People drifted in and out of the bar's entrance at the back, chattering to one another. Wisps of cigarette smoke and maybe even a little weed floated toward him. Winslow paused to breathe in.

He stood, hidden in the shadows, uncertain if he wanted to venture inside. He knew what he'd find—people having fun, dancing, drinking, playing pool and darts, and flirting. Normal stuff. Stuff he should have felt a part of, given his age. And yet, and yet...he couldn't shake the feeling of separation and isolation that refused to leave him, even when the melody of the anthem "Everybody Dance Now" reached his ears. Despite being at a gathering spot that had the expressed purpose of bringing people together, Winslow was apart, isolated.

He was only twenty-seven, but he felt like he had fifty years on all of those carefree folks, as though he'd left his youth behind when he'd taken up with Chad. He'd surrendered body and soul to the man. And what had he gotten in return? Bruises? Scrapes? Cowering when someone raised a voice?

Someone spoke from behind him. The voice was deep with a velvety quality. "First time?"

He turned to see a gorgeous black man, about the same age as Winslow, a lopsided grin lighting up his face. His hair was twisted into dreadlocks that fell over his shoulders. He wore a simple white tank top and a pair of dark jeans. Even in the dark, there was a twinkle in his eyes, as though the irises had captured the moon's pale luminescence above them. He'd shoved his hands into his front pockets.

"Hardly." Winslow smiled. "Just not sure I'm in the mood."

The grin widened. "I thought maybe we were kindred spirits."

And that caused Winslow to smile at last. "So?" He cocked his head. "*Your* first time?"

He nodded. "First time at a gay bar, anyway." He whispered the words gay and bar even though there was no one nearby. There was no one within a mile's radius who would even care, for that matter. The guy's naivete was kind of sweet.

Neither made a move to go inside. "There's nothing to be afraid of," Winslow said. "I haven't been to the Q in a while, but when I did used to come here a bit more often, the crowd was always nice, welcoming. A lot of friendly faces. Little attitude. Mary Louise, the bartender, is especially sweet. She's like someone's mom. But don't tell her I said that." Winslow tried to let his posture, his demeanor and, most of all, his smile, convey that this guy had nothing to fear. "I'm Winslow, by the way."

They shook hands. "That's a nice name. I'm Darryn."

"You live in Hopewell?"

Darryn nodded. "Just up the road, honestly. With my ma. She's a god-fearing Christian woman—her words, not mine—and has been cursing this place as long as I can remember. Her Baptist roots tell her it's a hotbed of sin, a place where perverts and sodomites gather." He wiggled his eyebrows in a way that was both disarming and charming.

Winslow laughed. "If you're lucky."

Winslow moved the toe of his tennis shoe around in the gravel and then looked up and said something uncharacteristic for his shy self. "Tell you what, come inside with me, and I'll buy you your first drink in a gay bar. You'll always remember me for that."

Darryn didn't seem to need to ponder. "Okay."

And Winslow started toward the door. Just as he was about to open it, Darryn said, "Wait."

Winslow turned.

"I'm not ready."

"What do you mean? You look fine." And he did—there was something unaware in this guy, as though he was oblivious to his good bone structure, his broad shoulders, flat stomach, and endearing smile.

And his lack of awareness made him all the more attractive.

"I didn't mean how I look. I just don't know if I'm ready for this step."

Winslow had to resist the urge to tell him how adorable his reluctance was. He could remember being seventeen—with his badly faked ID—coming to the Q for the first time ten years ago. He was shocked they'd let him in. That night, he'd gotten drunk on sloe-gin fizzes and had his first—and worst ever—hangover the next day. Much of that night was still a blank in his memory. For example, he was ashamed and embarrassed that he had no idea to this day how he managed to get home and between his own sheets that night. At least he hadn't wound up in some stranger's bed.

He realized he might have made a mistake when sizing Darryn up. "How old *are* you, anyway?"

"I'm old enough to get in," Darryn answered, sounding defensive. "Don't worry. I wouldn't even know how to get a fake ID, even if I wanted one."

"I didn't mean that. I just assumed you were about the same age as I am, twenty-seven, but maybe I guessed wrong?"

Darryn chuckled. "I just turned twenty-one."

Winslow cocked his head, "Oh? When?"

Darryn cast his gaze downward, smiling shyly. "Today."

Winslow sucked in a breath. "Oh my god. It's your birthday! Your twenty-first! Happy birthday!" He laughed out of sheer delight. "Now, you have to let me buy you that drink."

Darryn stood still as though frozen to the ground.

"Come on," Winslow coaxed. "We can go in, have a cocktail or a beer, and check things out. And if you don't like it? We can leave. No problem, no pressure." He quickly corrected himself. "Or, rather, *you* can leave." Winslow smiled. "The *we* was awfully presumptive on my part." Winslow realized, without warning, that he wanted there to be a we, even if it was only as something to hold on to, a life preserver against a dark rising tide. Even if it was only for an hour or two.

"Well, okay. But just one. I'm not much of a drinker."

Winslow opened the door for Darryn and watched him go in first. Once the bouncer checked their IDs, they headed toward the bar.

Winslow asked, "What are we drinking, birthday boy?" He'd almost forgotten Chad and that was actually wonderful. Oblivion could be a very effective pain medication. But like all pain medications, it was important that one not overdo it.

Darryn didn't looked embarrassed in the least as he wondered, "Do you think this Mary Louise can whip up a sloe-gin fizz?"

Winslow smiled broader to conceal the rumbling in his tummy.

Chapter Fifteen

Would I Lie to You?

Sammy gave up. He'd tried texting Chris more times than he could count. He'd called and left numerous voice mails, each more pleading than the last. He'd even tried to call Andre, that asshole, so he could confront him about the little prank he'd played. He'd never cared much for Chris's best friend and found him to be hollow inside—a man who saw no further than the end of his own nose when it came to things like kindness and compassion. Concepts like devotion and fidelity weren't in Andre's vocabulary. This joke—if that's what it was—was typical of him, tasteless and sowing the seeds of discord.

Now, it was getting on toward ten o'clock and Sammy could think of nothing else to do other than get himself dressed and head out to the Q. It's where everyone went on a Saturday night and where he hoped to find Chris, with whom he could put things right. He was certain if he could just have a few words with him, face-to-face, Chris would understand and would see that

Sammy loved him, adored him, banked on a future with him.

Even though Sammy was a self-admitted horn dog and did enjoy porn and looking at other men, he really and truly had eyes for no one other than Chris, which is why he felt consumed by desolation and despair.

He didn't know what he'd do if he couldn't fix things.

And once he did fix things—and he simply had to—he'd take some sort of revenge on Andre. What the hell was the matter with him, anyway?

*

Sammy pulled over to the side of the road because he knew the parking lot would already be full.

He slipped from the car and walked toward the bar. In back of the squat cinder block building, people gathered, laughing, talking, smoking. A couple made out near the tree line. At first, Sammy thought they were two young guys, but then saw they were young women, both sporting almost identical outfits—baseball caps, ribbed tanks, and cargo shorts.

Another couple, this one most assuredly male, emerged awkwardly from the back of a gray sedan. The first was an older guy, good-looking, with messy salt-and-pepper hair, a shirt buttoned wrong, and a pair of jeans he was sheepishly zipping as he peered around, looking guilty.

Sammy stopped dead in his tracks when he saw the other person emerge from the back seat of the car.

Andre.

Of course, Andre didn't have a hair out of place. His dark jeans and crimson T-shirt fit his muscular form almost as if he'd spray-painted them on.

The older guy hurried away from the car without looking back. And Andre, like Sammy, stood frozen in place as his gaze locked with Sammy's.

Sammy drew in a deep breath. He wondered if he could trust himself not to channel his rage and lunge at the guy. He closed his eyes and whispered words his mama used to say all the time, "Lord, give me strength."

Andre had looked away and was heading back toward the bar entrance. He had a little spring in his step, which infuriated Sammy even more.

"Yo, Andre!" Sammy called.

Andre stopped, his shoulders hunched up a little. He didn't turn around.

"Not gonna say hello?" Sammy marched up behind him.

Andre turned slowly. Sure, he was a handsome guy, but the sheepish grin he'd plastered to his face did him no favors. He stood, facing Sammy, hands at his sides, and didn't say a word.

Keep your temper in check. Keep it in check. Sammy would try his best to listen to his best self, yet he blurted, "What the fuck, man? I mean, what the *fuck*?"

"What are you talking about?" There was a little quiver to his voice that told Sammy Andre knew exactly to what he was referring.

Andre cocked his head. "Please. You know exactly what I mean. What was up with that text you sent me?"

Andre waved his hand, as though banishing the text—and any culpability for sending it—to the wind. "It was just a joke."

"So, you don't deny sending it?"

"Nah, man. I thought it would be funny—that you guys would get a kick out of it."

"Well, we didn't. Do you know what actually happened?" Sammy told him how Chris had seen the obscene text while Sammy was in the shower and, quite logically, jumped to the wrong conclusion.

"That's on him, right?"

"No! No, it's not *on* him, Andre. It's on *you*. Never mind that I don't have you in my contacts, so it popped up without a name—"

Andre's snicker caused him to stop. Sammy was regularly a gentle soul, but he was *this close* to clocking this asshole. "It's not funny. Chris saw that and stormed out." Sammy looked down at the ground and then back up. It felt like a horde of bees swarmed inside. "I don't know where he is," he said softly.

"Oh, for Christ's sake. So now there's trouble in paradise? Excuse the fuck out of me." Andre stepped close, getting in Sammy's personal space. Sammy felt as though Andre was sucking the oxygen right out of the night air. "You know, if you guys were solid, Chris wouldn't have jumped to conclusions. He would have trusted you."

"What? So now, I'm to blame?"

Andre stared at him for a moment and then sighed. "I'm gonna get a drink. I'll buy you one. Peace offering."

"You're out of your mind. Just go away."

And that's exactly what Andre did. Sammy watched as he proceeded into the bar. He showed not even a smidgen of remorse or concern. How did he live with himself?

Sammy was ready to head back to the car, but then reminded himself that he should at least go inside and check. He doubted he'd find Chris there, but if he didn't at least take a quick look, he'd never know.

He discovered he was wrong as soon as he entered the bar. There was Chris, seated beneath a mirror on a carpet-covered bench built out from the wall. He clutched a bottle of beer in one hand and, for all the world, looked like the saddest soul on the planet.

No wonder no one was near him. His sadness could be catching, especially in a place that was all about cutting loose, celebrating, and maybe, finding the *one*.

Chris was the *one*.

Sammy edged closer, feeling an irrational fear as though he'd actually cheated. Finally, he stood right in front of Chris, who took a second to realize it because he was so absorbed in the color, perhaps, of the beer in the bottle he clutched so hard in his hand his knuckles were white.

"Chris?" Sammy said softly.

He looked up. For a moment, a smile flickered across his features and even something else, relief perhaps. And then, like a curtain being drawn, his face closed up, right before Sammy's eyes.

"What are you doing here?" Chris asked. His voice was cold, and his gaze was somewhere beyond Sammy.

"I came to find you." Sammy sat on the bench, but not too close. Not yet. He swallowed and added, "I thought we were coming out together. Did I get that wrong?"

Chris took a long swallow of his beer and stared off into space for agonizing moments. When he finally spoke, he asked, "What's going on?"

Sammy was relieved, actually, that he'd broached the subject, however obliquely. "You mean about the text?"

Chris simply stared at him. At least he was meeting his eye.

Sammy leaned closer. "I know this sounds like what every cheater says when they get caught, but it wasn't what it looked like."

Chris smirked.

Sammy shook his head. "Uh-uh. That's not a good look on you."

"What do you mean?"

"That disbelief on your face. That judgment. Do you want me to be honest with you or not?"

Chris took a while to respond to that too. "Of course, I want you to be honest. But I don't know if I can *believe* you." When he looked at Sammy, there was such sorrow in his eyes that it nearly broke Sammy's heart.

Sammy searched the crowd until he found Andre, standing near the bar, sipping what looked like a gin and tonic. Pointing to him, he said, "See that guy?"

Chris followed his pointing finger. "Sure. Andre, you mean?"

"Yes. Andre." Sammy paused for a moment and then blurted out the truth. "He sent the text."

Even in the relative darkness of the club, Sammy watched Chris pale. "Oh, come on. You're fooling around with Andre? He wouldn't do that to me. We've known each other forever!"

Sammy laughed and felt a depth of despair he didn't know he had in him. "*He* wouldn't do that to you? What about me?" Sammy couldn't resist—he lightly took Chris's chin in his hand and turned Chris's face toward his own. "*I* would never do that to you. I *didn't* do that to you. Andre sent the text as some sort of sick joke. I don't see the humor in it, and I don't think you do either. You know what I think? What I really believe? It was no joke."

"What was it then?"

Was Chris opening up a little? Letting his defenses down?

Sammy wasn't sure if it was wishful thinking or not, but, oh, how he wanted to believe he was getting somewhere. "Honestly, I believe he's jealous of what we have. He wanted to cause trouble. And he did. But we don't have to let the trouble last for long. He's pathetic. I'm sorry. I know he's your friend, but come on, who does that?"

"Really?"

"Yes, really. I told you where I was on Tuesday." Sammy dug in his pocket for his iPhone. Once he had it in hand, he began scrolling, forefinger flicking rapidly on the screen. "Ah! Here it is."

He handed the phone to Chris, knowing what he'd see—a message from his dear friend, Brenda, telling him how her grandma had passed and she couldn't reach her sponsor. She had bought a bottle of Tanqueray, but hadn't opened it yet. Would Sammy come over and stop her from doing something she'd regret? And, of course, Sammy, having been in her shoes, had replied that he'd be there as soon as he could be.

Chris stared hard at the screen for what seemed like an eternity. And then he simply handed the phone back to Sammy.

Sammy waited. And when he could wait no longer, he asked, "You're not going to say anything?"

When Chris looked over at him, tears glistened in his eyes, ready to fall. "I'm sorry. I should have known."

Sammy gathered Chris in his arms, held him tightly. He could feel the repressed sobs coursing through Chris's body. *None of this had to happen.* "It's okay. What were you to think?"

Chris pulled away. "What was I to think? How about that I have, for the first time ever, a good man in my life who loves me and that maybe I should have trusted him instead of flying off the handle?"

Sammy shook his head. "You're human, sweetheart. We all make mistakes. I might have made the same one if the tables were turned." That last part was a lie. Sammy would have gotten to the bottom of things, immediately. He would not have gone for the explanation that Chris was cheating on him, no matter how incriminating or filthy a text could prove to be. But he wouldn't tell him that.

He'd gotten through to Chris. He knew Chris believed.

Chris wiped his nose on the back of his hand. "Sorry. That's disgusting." He then rubbed his hand on his shorts.

"I love you, Chris Patterson. Snot and all."

Chris laughed. "What did I do to deserve you?"

"All you had to do, honey, was show up. Let's put this behind us. Let's have a drink, go home, and get crazy.

All night long..." Sammy gave Chris what he hoped was his most winning smile.

"That sounds good." Chris sighed and leaned back against the wall. "You know what else I'm going to put behind me?"

Sammy hoped for a dirty response to the question, but Chris pointed to Andre. "Him. I'm going to put him behind me. Friendships run their course, and when you can see that the person you thought was your friend is no friend at all, when it's proven beyond a shadow, then you know it's time to move on. I'm just sorry it took this mess to wake me up to him."

"Are you mad at him?"

"That's the funny thing. I'm not. My heart actually aches for him because I've known—for a long time—that he's sad. He wants what we have, and underneath all the swinging and open relationship bravado, he's empty. And, if he can't have something like our relationship, he decided to see if he could take it away from me. It would be a win-win, you know? He could break us up and get me all to himself with one swoop." Chris shook his head. "All he did was alienate me."

"Ah, have a think about it," Sammy was surprised to hear himself saying. "Maybe you can talk it out, find forgiveness."

"Oh, I'll forgive him and maybe I already have. But I do that for me, not him. Sometimes, with people, one wrong word, one wrong action, can change everything because they display who they really are. And, after that, there's no going back."

Chris eyed him. "Can we just go home?"

Sammy stood and took Chris's hand. "Of course we can. Home is the only place I want to be—with you."

Chapter Sixteen

Right Here Waiting

When Gracie Fuentes came into the bar late, close to midnight, Mary Louise set down the beer mug she was drying on the drainer and let out a solitary "Oh."

Gracie was a study in despair. Her clothes, a worn flannel shirt and jeans, looked as though she'd slept in them. There was a stain on the shirt. The jeans were too long and dragged on the floor. Gracie's salt and pepper hair was smashed down in back. As she came closer, Mary Louise saw she was still holding a cigarette—but Gracie was oblivious to it. It had burned down to the filter between her fingers.

Her eyes were wild.

Billy had told Mary Louise what had happened earlier—Rose and Liz had been on their way to the Q when something—most likely a deer darting into the road—had caused them to swerve and then veer off into the trunk of a huge old maple tree. "It was bad, Mary Louise, really bad," Billy had reported. Mary Louise was surprised to see tears standing in his eyes. Billy Breedlove was the most unemotional man she'd ever known.

She remembered how sick she felt in her gut when he'd delivered the news in hushed tones over the bar. She'd been certain in that moment that both women were dead. The road to the Q had seen many accidents over the years; many of them had been fatal.

But she loved the "girls" as she called them. Simply watching them on the dance floor, shimmying and shaking to the latest dance sensation, always brought a smile to her face. And Gracie's not-so-hidden crush on Rose was kind of sweet in its own way—something rare in these days of online hooking up. It was old-fashioned, innocent. Hopelessly romantic. *If only I could inspire such devotion...*

Mary Louise held back the splash of bile she felt at the back of her throat and asked Billy, "They're gone, aren't they?" She imagined one of them impaled on the steering wheel, one propelled like a bullet through the windshield, lying among desiccated leaves and pine needles.

She didn't know how she could go on tonight if her suspicions were true. How could she serve people? Smile and banter with them?

It was simple. She'd close the bar. Rose and Liz would be owed at least that much.

But Billy shook his head. "They were both rushed to the hospital—in Wheeling. From what I understand, Liz is in a bad way. She's in a coma."

"And Rose?" Mary Louise's words trembled.

"She's banged up, but I heard she'll be okay. They'll probably keep her overnight for observation, but she should be released in the morning."

"Thank god," Mary Louise whispered, getting a little strength back in her knees. Her heart started to beat again.

And now, a couple hours later, Gracie approached the bar. The third member of the trio—the saddest one because Mary Louise sensed she wanted to be in a duo. And, right now, the sadness in her eyes radiated outward.

"Gracie! Have you seen them?" Without waiting for an answer, Mary Louise hurried around from behind the bar and took Gracie in her arms and squeezed her tight. Gracie stayed motionless, and Mary Louise moved away. "Have you?"

Gracie nodded, but the despair she'd displayed upon entering the bar was replaced by a kind of numb expression. She had already spent all her emotion and was poised to break down. Whatever it was, Mary Louise made an internal promise she'd be there for her.

"And? Billy said they're both in the hospital. They're gonna be okay, right? They'll patch 'em up, huh?"

Gracie's lower lip quivered, and she let out a single choked sob and then sucked in a breath. "Liz isn't gonna make it. They have her on life support, but they're just waiting for her brother to come down from Youngstown to take her off."

The words hung in the air—so simple, yet so devastating.

"Oh no," Mary Louise said, taking Gracie by the shoulders. "No. There's really no hope?"

Gracie stepped back so Mary Louise's arms fell from her shoulders. "They wouldn't do it if there was." She tapped her forehead with two fingers, looking sadder than a human being had a right to. "Brain dead."

"Shit. I guess they wouldn't take her off life support if there was any chance." Mary Louise pulled out a stool and guided Gracie onto it. Even in the dim dance-hall light of the bar, she looked pale, beaten down, shattered. She returned to the back of the bar and poured a shot of Jameson's into a glass and slid it toward Gracie, but Gracie only stared at it.

"And Rose?"

There was a flicker of something that moved across Gracie's careworn features. Relief? Hope? Maybe even joy? Gracie was not as easy to read tonight.

"Rose is gonna be okay. I'm gonna head back to the hospital and hang out with her tonight and then bring her back to my place in the morning. She broke her collarbone, and she's banged up bad, so I figure she can stay with me until she's more on the mend, you know?" Gracie picked up the shot glass and stared at it. She returned it to its place on the bar.

Mary Louise nodded. "You're a pal, Gracie. A real good friend."

The comment, meant to reassure and compliment, seemed to make Gracie even sadder. "That's me. A pal." She shoved the glass back across the bar. "You forgot, hon. I don't drink. Not anymore."

Mary Louise picked up the glass and eyed her. "Right. Club soda with lime, then?"

"Nah. I'm driving." She chuckled.

Mary Louise wanted to slap herself. "Sure you are. That was stupid of me to even offer."

Gracie said nothing as a long moment passed. "It's okay, Mary Louise. Your heart was in the right place. I get it."

"Just not my brain."

Gracie laughed and that was good to see—a soothing balm on Mary Louise's heart. In that moment, she recognized how much she cared about the people that came into the Q week after week. She might not see them much outside the confines of this sad, cinder block building, but she loved them all.

Gracie stood. "I need to get back to the hospital. I just, uh, wanted to stop by here and let you know. I figured there'd be talk. And I know you—you'd worry." Gracie, her shoulders stooped, trudged toward the exit. Mary Louise imagined her lack of hope, her despair. *We need to let people know what they mean to us. We never know when too late might arrive on our doorstep.*

"Gracie?" Mary Louise called out.

Gracie turned, her face expectant.

Mary Louise gave her a smile. She hoped her caring and sympathy were summed up in that small expression. "Come back here a minute."

Gracie moved back toward the bar. "I really need to get to the hospital."

Mary Louise ignored Gracie's impatience and said, "Tell her."

Gracie shook her head. "What do you mean?"

"For the love of god, woman, just *tell her*."

Mary Louise could read the understanding on Gracie's face, and yet, for some reason, she didn't want to admit she knew.

"It's no secret, hon, except maybe from you and Rose." Mary Louise laughed.

Gracie sighed.

"You know what I'm talking about. Just tell her, okay?"

"Okay." Gracie turned.

"Tell Rose you love her. Everyone can see it." Mary Louise reached out her hand. It hung in the air for a minute, and then she let it drop back to her side. "If you learn one thing from this terrible accident, it's that none of us knows how much time we have."

Gracie stood, frozen, halfway between the bar now and the exit. Behind her impassive face, wheels turned. "You're right, Mary Louise. You're always right."

"I don't know about *that*," Mary Louise said. "But I am right about this, and you know it. So will you please tell Rose that I love her and that *you* do too."

Gracie smiled and nodded.

And then she was gone.

Chapter Seventeen

Go Your Own Way

Ralph and Donna had been sitting at the bar, a couple seats down from Mary Louise and Gracie as they'd had their exchange about time running out, about admitting love.

Their talk made Ralph feel unreasonably sad. Of course, Mary Louise had been right. It had been a standing joke at the Q for years—the great unrequited passion Gracie had for Rose. Would they never get a clue? Or was Liz interfering too much? Did she have her own designs on Rose?

The questions weren't Ralph's to answer. He gazed down into his whiskey and soda and stirred the little red plastic straw around in the melting ice cubes. *Why did that little exchange hit me in the gut? Why do I care if a couple lesbians find their happy ending?* The questions taunted Ralph in the back of his mind. But the answers to them were no mystery.

He knew why.

There was a big difference between contentment and happiness. It was like the difference between fish sticks and filet mignon—both were good, but only one felt like a celebration instead of just sustenance, a meal. *Oh, cut it with the metaphors, Ralph. They're weak. You would have given a student who came up with one like you just thought of a barely passing grade back in the day.*

Ralph pulled the straw from his drink and set it on the bar. He lifted the whiskey to his lips and chugged what remained in the glass. His putting it back down caught Donna's attention.

She swiveled her stool a little more toward him. "You want another one? It's my turn to buy."

Ralph was confused. *Why is there a ball in my throat? Why do my eyes burn?* He looked at Donna's face, a face he loved, with all its laugh lines and crow's feet. It was still the face of a beautiful woman. And he could see his own love for her reflected back in her wide brown eyes.

He thought of being an adolescent boy alone in his room, playing his very first record album on the record player that topped his dresser. The album? Carole King's *Tapestry*. God, he'd listened to that album so many times that even now, a half century later, he still remembered the words to every song on it. He could see the lyrics on the back of the album in his mind's eye, printed over a background of tapestry fabric.

The song that came to mind at the moment was the most mournful one, "It's Too Late." Although it was about the embers of a love winking out, leaving ash and regret in their wake, Ralph wondered if it was ever truly too late to find the happiness one sought.

He thought he'd given up a long time ago on things like passion, lust, joy, and the simple lifting of his heart. Donna was great. He did love her with a deep, undeniable affection. He loved her as one loves a pair of comfy, fleece-lined slippers, or chocolate cupcakes, or watching the first flurries of snow at the start of winter. All good, but...

But there was no spark.

There never had been. They'd both said, more than once, they knew that going in.

And as sure as Ralph was of this truth for himself, he was sure of it for Donna too.

She waved her fingers at him, giggling. "Hello? Ground control to Major Tom?"

Oh, they had so much in common! They were one of those couples who could easily finish each other's sentences. Their inside jokes could fill a doorstop-sized volume.

So why did he feel like breaking into sobs right now?

"Sorry, sweetheart." Ralph looked down at his empty glass, but couldn't find his voice to answer. Yes, he did want another, but no...

"Don't you want another Seagrams?" Donna took a sip of her own drink—a Diet Coke. The number of alcoholic drinks Donna had consumed in her life Ralph could count on one hand. "It's not that I don't approve, or I'm some teetotaler, I just don't like the taste," she'd told him many years ago.

When Ralph didn't reply, Donna asked, "Or do you just want to go home? Get into our jammies? I just got a shipment from Amazon of decaf Earl Grey." Donna grinned, expecting him to go along with her.

And, without warning, it just seemed so *sad*—two people whose passions lay elsewhere settling for a watered-down excuse for a marriage. Admitting that didn't diminish the value of what they had, of course. Donna would always be a part of his heart. She'd forever mean as much to him as any family member, even his saint of a mother, gone for so many years, stolen from him by lung cancer.

"What are we doing?" he asked, wincing at how broken and defeated his voice sounded.

Donna's eyebrows, thick, furrowed together above her tortoiseshell glasses frame. "What do you mean, hon?" She laughed, but there was an uncertainty to it. "We're having drinks. Getting out among folks."

She knows.

She gets exactly what I mean. She just doesn't want to hear it.

She shook her head. "We need to get you home," she said quickly. "I think Ralphie here has had a little too much. We'll get you into bed, and then I'll make your favorite in the morning."

She didn't have to name his favorite, of course, because they both knew it so well—four-minute eggs broken overtop crumbled up and heavily-buttered toast. Lots of salt and pepper.

Her face was innocent. He doubted he could hurt her more if he raised his fist and slugged her. The promise of flannel pajamas and a hot cup of milky Earl Grey was tempting but not tempting enough for him to *not* say words he'd never said in their many years of coming out together at the Q. "Darling, why don't you go on ahead? I can tell you're tired. I think I'd like to stay awhile."

Donna simply stared. There was confusion on her plain but pretty face. Hurt, maybe, too. She cocked her head. "But, but how will *you* get home? We came in my car."

"I know. And I'll be okay—I'm a big boy. Even out here in the sticks, there are cabs and Ubers. Besides, a good Samaritan might give me a lift as well. I'll get home if that's what's worrying you. Safe and in one piece." He smiled. "And we can have those soft-boiled eggs in the morning."

But could they? Would they? This was a turning point, and Ralph could make light of it, or he could own up to it.

Donna stiffened but made no attempt to move. "That's not really what I'm worried about."

"Worry? Oh, you have nothing to worry about!"

She cocked her head. "Don't I?" She swirled around the dregs in her tall glass. "Why, Ralph? Why now? Why don't you want me to stay? For so many years, you and I have come out together to this bar on Saturday night and never once have we not arrived together and not once have we not left together."

"Maybe I need to try something new. They say change is a good thing."

The words hung in the air, shards. Ralph almost wished he hadn't spoken them aloud. He knew Donna was hurt and feeling excluded.

"Maybe you need to try *someone* new." Donna's voice was barely above a whisper. She slid from her stool without looking at him, turned, and walked from the bar. She stumbled a little as she reached the exit, then righted herself.

Ralph watched, heart in his throat, until she was out the door. Gone. He tried to tell himself this was no big thing. But it was. It really was. Ralph knew this was a line in the sand they'd both always remember crossing, no matter what the rest of the night held.

He ached.

Yet he raised his hand and gave Mary Louise a little wave. "Can I get another? And could you make this one a double?"

Part Three

You Don't Have to Go Home

But You Can't Stay Here

Chapter Eighteen

My Father's Eyes

Riccardo eyed Nels DiCarlo from a discreet distance.

The bouncer, a blond with tattoos and piercings who reminded Riccardo of Mickey Rourke in the movie from a few years back, *The Wrestler*, had pointed him out when the bartender refused to let him in on who exactly was the mysterious Mr. DiCarlo.

What Riccardo saw was an older man, still handsome, wearing well-fitting dark jeans, a pale-blue Oxford button-down, and black Chuck Taylors. He looked youthful and hip without trying. He was handsome in a craggy sort of way, with mostly gray hair and warm dark eyes. Riccardo could imagine that he would look much the same, given twenty years or so. They had the same strong bone structure, the same eyes, even some of the same gestures. Riccardo wondered why he was alone and if he was here tonight to try to remedy that.

Was his dad a slut? A bar fly?

Riccardo didn't think so. The man sipping his Rolling Rock (the same beer Riccardo was drinking) at the bar had an air of quiet dignity. There was also an aloofness, a sense of being apart, that Riccardo found oddly sad and endearing. It was as though DiCarlo didn't quite fit here. Although he certainly didn't appear to think he was above the humble confines of the bar, he was *apart*.

Maybe that's why he was alone. Maybe that's why, since Riccardo had observed him, he'd made little conversation with anyone beyond simple pleasantries.

Riccardo still wasn't sure he wanted to approach him. To do so was like throwing a hand grenade into a calm and settled building.

Who knew how the guy would react? Riccardo was filled suddenly with doubts about his plan. Did he really have the right to upset this man's life? To what end? It wasn't like Riccardo expected much. He'd grown up with two wonderful parents, and the memory of their love sustained him. And his own wife and kid on the way? Weren't they enough? Why was he going forward with this harebrained scheme? Who would benefit?

You've come all this way. You're just scared. You're here for a reason. Good or bad, you can leave here tonight with something more than you had, even if it's simply the knowledge of each other. Even if it's just opening a door a crack. At least there's a chance. There's hope. And that baby on the way? A grandpa might be a nice gift one of these days.

Riccardo, back in high school, had thought he'd like, one day, to be an actor. Everyone told him he had the looks, the bearing, the voice for it. He always landed the leads in any high school productions that didn't involve singing. The adage about not being able to carry a tune in a bucket applied to him. It always struck his friends as odd—his lack of singing ability, with his father touring all over the world in operatic productions.

Anyway, the moment he was experiencing right now was akin to being backstage in the wings, waiting to go on. There was a sense of dread wedded with a ticklish feeling of anticipation. It was an unlikely yet potent cocktail. And there was nothing else to do really, once you heard your cue out there under the bright lights, but to take a deep breath and step out from behind the curtain.

Riccardo took a deep breath now, told himself there was no turning back, and approached Nelson DiCarlo. He stood behind him for only a moment—because he didn't want to come across as some creepy stalker—and then tapped him on the shoulder.

Nelson DiCarlo gave a little start, then swiveled his stool to turn and face him.

There was a quiet moment as Nelson appraised Riccardo. Their gazes locked. It wasn't a romantic moment, of course, but it was an intimate one. Without a word spoken, there was a connection.

Nelson opened his mouth as though to speak and then closed it again. He summoned a smile.

"Mr. DiCarlo, you don't know me—" Riccardo began.

Nelson held up a hand to interrupt. "Let me stop you right there, son." Even under the dim lighting conditions, Riccardo watched the man's cheek color at the use of the word *son*. Freudian slip? Or did he already know who Riccardo was? "I know who you are."

So the bartender must have not only made good on her promise to let Nelson know who he was but maybe pointed him out as well. "You do?"

Nelson nodded and then waved a hand toward the bartender. "Mary Louise told me you were looking for me." Nelson took a sip of his beer. Not a lot, but his hand shook a bit as he raised the bottle to his lips. "It's been quite the night for revelations. If you only knew!" He set his beer back down. "But Mary Louise didn't tell me your name. And that's a fine place, I think, for us to start." He extended his hand. "Nelson DiCarlo, but everyone just calls me Nels."

"Riccardo." He shook Nels's hand, unsure about giving his last name because it was associated with fame.

Nels didn't press him on the last name. He did tap the person's arm sitting next to him—a redheaded guy in camo pants and a white wifebeater—and asked if he wouldn't mind scooting down so "my friend and I can catch up."

The guy had no problem. In fact, he picked up his Bud Lite and completely wandered away.

Riccardo sat.

"Can I get you another beer?"

"Yeah, that would be nice. Thanks."

Nels took care of ordering, and in no time, there was a new green bottle in front of Riccardo. Once that little task was accomplished, though, silence fell. Surprisingly, Riccardo hadn't thought things through—he'd been too excited at the simple prospect of coming face to face with this man.

"So?" Nels began. "Mary Louise over there tells me you're claiming to be my son."

Oh great. This is where he disputes me. Tells me I have the wrong guy...or the wrong gay. This is where he says I couldn't possibly be his because he's never been with a woman nor has he ever had occasion to donate sperm.

But that's not what happened. "How did you find me?"

Riccardo explained about the DNA test and how, quite unexpectedly, he'd gotten the surprising result of knowing his biological father.

"I took one of those tests too. Wasn't too sure about it, but it was, like, a year ago. Never been back to check out new matches."

Riccardo nodded. "I know this comes as a shock, and I want to say right up front that I want nothing special from you. I just wanted to meet you."

"You really believe I'm the right guy?"

Riccardo gestured toward the big mirror over the bar and leaned closer, so their faces were side by side in reflection. "Look at that," Riccardo said softly.

"Beauty and the beast." Nels snickered. "No, no, I see what you mean." Nels removed his gaze from the reflection to look into Riccardo's eyes. "There's definitely a resemblance."

"Are you surprised?"

"More than you know. But it works out. This may be TMI, but I've only had sex with a woman once, and the dates would add up, if you were born around fall of 1978."

"October 22," Riccardo said, heart pounding faster.

Nels nodded. "We can verify this."

"Of course."

"But in my gut, I'm sure you're right." Nels's gaze roved over Riccardo. "Although I must say you're like the perfect version of me that even I couldn't attain when I was your age."

Riccardo didn't really know what to say. What words does one use in a situation like this, anyway? He blurted, "I'd like us to get to know each other."

"Oh, I'd love that, Riccardo." Nels nodded. "I'd love that very much." He cocked his head. "Do you live around here?"

"New York. Chelsea? About six hours away by car. Not all that far. I grew up on the Upper West Side of Manhattan."

"Fancy."

Riccardo wasn't about to be falsely modest. His upbringing *had* been fancy—their condo was worth a couple million easy. He'd gone to private schools and had taken his first trip to Paris when he was just three years old. He'd seen Nels's humble house. This wasn't the time to bring up things like his parents' wealth or fame. "It's okay. My adoptive parents gave me a good life. I never wanted for a thing."

"I'm glad to hear it."

Nels paused for a long time, and Riccardo could see he was considering something. "Do you believe in fate? Or at least in truth-is-stranger-than-fiction coincidences?"

"Sometimes, sure." Riccardo wasn't sure what he was getting at.

"Earlier tonight, your mother was here."

Riccardo burst into laughter. He doubled over with it. Tears came to his eyes. As he tried to straighten up and catch his breath, he saw Nels looking at him strangely. He thought he had the laughter under control and then another fit coursed through him, ticklish and giddy.

Nelson chuckled, but asked, "What?" He was genuinely mystified.

Riccardo let out a big breath. "Oh! I'm sorry. I'm sorry. It's just that—what did you say?"

"About your mother being here earlier tonight?"

"That was the one. You were kidding, right? I mean, that would simply be too much of a coincidence."

Nels thought for a moment. "You know, real life is often filled with coincidences that would never fly in a book or movie. But I've seen enough of these weird happenstances to believe in fate, to believe that, maybe, just maybe—for better or worse—things are unfolding according to some master plan."

He drank some more beer and stifled a belch with the back of his hand. "Pardon me. No, I wasn't kidding. She was here. Her name is Cathy Corak. And you won't believe this, but she told me about you."

"No."

"Yes. I hadn't seen Cathy since high school. Ready to have your mind blown a little more?" Nelson grinned, but there was something else in his face that Riccardo couldn't put a finger on. Panic, maybe? Hysteria?"

"Okay." Riccardo reached out a hand to steady himself against the bar.

"I haven't seen Cathy in over forty years. And tonight, about two hours ago, she waltzes in, smelling of the '70s and lays a shocker on me—from our one and only encounter in the front seat of her mother's car, we produced a kid. You." Nelson squinted. "You sure you're over forty?"

"Just. Don't remind me."

Riccardo felt an urge to flee. He wanted to know more, needed to know more, but right now, this unexpected turn was too much for his fragile psyche to bear. He longed for the warmth of his bed in New York, spooning with Maya, feeling the squirming, kicking life in her belly. Part of him wished he'd never opened this door because it was making him confused. He wondered what he'd missed and then wondered: *Would I have been better off simply not knowing? Is this a Pandora's Box?*

After they were silent for a long while, Nels must have intuited Riccardo's discomfort because he leaned over to whisper, "Too much?"

Riccardo let slip another small chuckle. "Maybe a little. I mean, I was ready to meet *you*, but not all the rest. My wife told me I didn't know what I was walking into." He gazed around the bar. It was getting late, and the crowd of revelers was thinning. Those who did remain were like wilting flowers—a little worse for the wear. "Is she here?"

"Nah. She disappeared into the night like a ghost. But the good news? We exchanged numbers. If you want, maybe you can meet her. Of course, she'd also have to want to meet you—that goes without saying, but I'm pretty sure she will."

Riccardo wasn't sure how to respond. He felt sick to his stomach. He couldn't have anticipated the queasiness. *Shouldn't I be excited? Thrilled? Two parents for the price of one. How did I get so lucky?*

"She told me she gave you up for adoption right after you were born." Nels went on to explain how Cathy was in town for her mother's funeral and just thought it was time Nels knew they'd created a life together. "But what are the odds, huh? That we'd all end up here tonight?"

"Astronomical." Riccardo felt a little weak. His fight or flight response was firmly on the flight path. He wanted to turn and run from the bar, hole up in his motel room, and get the hell back to NYC the next day, where things were safe.

What had he been thinking?

He'd brought this on himself, but it didn't change the fact that he felt like he'd landed in an episode of *The Twilight Zone*. He didn't say anything for a long while, and then he asked, "What's she like?"

Nels considered the question for a moment. Then he squeezed Riccardo's shoulder and the gesture filled Riccardo with warmth, as though something had been imparted from Nels into the very muscles of his shoulders.

"Please," he said softly and didn't quite understand why.

Nels cocked his head and then answered. "Like I said, I haven't seen her in over forty years. I'll tell you this—she's a good person. I can feel that about someone right off. I sensed it about her back when we were kids, and I sense it about you now. I'm never wrong about first impressions. I believe they come to me for a reason. I think our instinct, our guts, our heart—whatever you choose to call them—always tells the truth. We just have to listen." He took a sip of beer. "Honestly? My take is that, even though she's a good person, kind, good-hearted, she's broken. From what little I could gather, she's had a tough time of things. I'll let her tell you details if you guys choose to meet up. And that's on her as much as it is on you, but I suspect she'll be thrilled to finally meet you and see what a fine man you turned out to be.

"Cathy was troubled even in school. She was not the kind of person I hung around with. Hell, I hung around with hardly anyone. For the most part, I was the kid that got beat up for his lunch money. But, like you, I was cute. So the girls, including Cathy, were interested. We weren't together for long—ships passing in the night. A couple dates. Our circles didn't really intersect. I was a loner, and she wanted to be loved. By anyone."

Riccardo watched Nels cast his gaze down at the bar. He wondered if Nels was catching himself, grabbing back those words—*by anyone*—regretting their meaning. So what if his biological mother got around?

"I'm sorry. I probably know your real mother about as well as you do. And what I said about her willing to be loved by anyone? I meant it in the romantic self. Cathy had a reputation back in high school, but it appears it wasn't deserved."

"My real mother passed away."

Nels put his hand on Riccardo's arm. The touch, again, was electric. "I'm sorry. Of course your real mother is the woman who raised you. Same with your real father. The *parents* you have here? We were just a couple of kids fumbling around in the dark in an old Valiant. Your conception probably took all of a minute." He chuckled. "Sorry if that's TMI, but it's the truth. We both contributed genetic material to you, and that was it."

"But blood means something, doesn't it? Genes?" Riccardo asked.

Nels shrugged. "I don't know, honestly. Is that a nature versus nurture kind of question?" He didn't wait for Riccardo to respond, and Riccardo wasn't even sure if he'd posed the question as anything other than rhetorical. "I think those have to mean something. I mean, do you feel the same as I do? We've known each other only for a few moments, really, and yet I feel a kinship with you, both literally and figuratively." He didn't speak for a long while. When he finally did, he appeared almost timid, afraid. "I debated whether to say this. But what have I got to lose?"

Riccardo smiled. "What?" And then he watched as Nels's eyes shimmered with tears.

Nels wiped them quickly away. "This will sound bizarre..." Nels took in a deep breath and eyed Riccardo, looked away, looked back. "But I love you."

The words hung in the air.

Riccardo wasn't sure what to say, how to respond. The words were the last thing he expected to hear. Could this man love him in the space of a few minutes, really love him? His head said no, but his heart nudged him along, saying softly, *yes. Stranger things have happened. I fell in love with Maya when I first saw her coming out of the subway station on Broadway near Zabars. And yes, when she first told me she was pregnant, I immediately loved that little life even though I've yet to lay eyes on my little boy.* Riccardo breathed in, out. *There's your answer.*

It turned out he needn't have been too concerned about what to say in response to Nels's declaration. He was literally saved by the bell. His iPhone rang in his pocket. He held up a finger. "Sorry, I should take this." He looked down at the screen and saw Maya was calling. "I *really* need to take this."

He hopped from the stool and hurried away from Nels, dodging his way through the crowd. He got outside just in time to answer her call before it went to voice mail. "Honey?"

"Ah, so glad I got hold of you."

"It's late. Is everything okay?"

"Well…" her voice trailed off. Maya could be a bit of a drama queen, and Riccardo figured she was building suspense. "It seems a certain someone is coming earlier than expected."

"The baby?" Riccardo shouted in a voice made higher by excitement.

"No, Tiny Fey."

"What?"

Maya chuckled. "Yes, the baby. Our son. Tate."

"Where are you now?"

"I'm at the hospital with Mom. All is well. They say it looks like I have a few hours to go. I'm only dilated a couple centimeters. Right now, no big deal, but I'm sure that's all gonna change."

It was so late, but he had to get home. "Do you think I can make it back in time?"

"Yeah, maybe. If you're lucky with getting a flight out of there."

"I'll go back to the hotel right now and see what I can do." The flight from Pittsburgh to New York was only a little more than an hour. If he could grab a red-eye or early morning flight, there was reasonable hope he could make it back in time to be there for the birth of his son.

"You do that. I'll do my best to keep the little one inside. Kidding!"

He heard voices in the background, and then Maya said, "Listen, Mom just walked back in, so I'm gonna hang up. Call me back when you have an ETA, okay?"

"Okay," Riccardo said. And then he added, "I love you," but Maya had already hung up.

He'd started toward the parking lot and his rental when he realized he should at least say something to Nels. He hurried back inside and made his way over to where he still sat at the bar.

Nels looked a little abashed as he asked, "Is everything okay?"

"Yeah, everything's better than okay, actually." He told him about the call and the baby now on its way.

"That's wonderful! I'm so happy for you."

"Give me your phone." Riccardo held out his hand and, when Nels handed him the phone, entered his number. "This is so you can reach me. Drop me a text or something so I have your number, okay?" He handed the phone back. "I gotta run, but I'll let you know about the baby." Although he didn't want to say "I love you" back, he could at least tell the man when his grandson made an entrance into the world.

"Thank you!" Nels said.

Riccardo hurried out into the humid night. *What an experience this has been. And it's only the beginning...*

Chapter Nineteen

Hello, It's Me

It was late, almost two in the morning, when Nels stumbled from his driveway to the back door of his house. Crickets chirped and the wind caused the leaves in the big maple in his front yard to whisper to one another. They gave Nels no clues to their secrets.

Other than the hum of insects and the wind, the night was silent. He breathed in the night, gazed up at the stars for a moment. It was cooling off with dawn's approach.

The quiet, though, was broken as Nels neared his back door, which led into the kitchen. It was Homer, making a ruckus. The little dog barked and scratched on the worn back door. Nels knew he'd decided he'd been left alone too long. As it was every time Nels left the house for more than a few minutes, Homer's heart was broken, certain he'd be left alone forever.

Nels grinned and rolled his eyes. All he wanted to do right now was fall into bed, to sleep and perchance to dream—of a son and a grandson. How could his world have changed so completely in the space of a few hours?

Having a dog meant you were never really free.

Make no mistake, Homer was worth any extra work or trouble he required. Nels wouldn't trade the little dog for the world. The love and companionship he selflessly gave were invaluable. But sometimes, much as he loved the little guy, Nels longed for a break. Dogs were children that never grew up. He sighed, got out his keys, and opened the door.

Homer rushed out between his legs, panting, whining, and barking. He jumped on Nels again and again, ricocheting off his calves. Although he only weighed about twenty pounds, his excitement carried a lot of force. He almost knocked Nels over, totally boisterous, even though it was the wee small hours of the morning. Nels laughed and felt a little lift in his energy. This was why he had a dog, despite the demands—the unconditional love and Homer's absolute joy whenever he came home. He was neither too old, too boring, or too lonely for Homer. He was everything—and a bag of chicken treats.

Homer quickly raced off toward the backyard, where he lifted his leg on a lilac bush and then sniffed around for a bit.

Give the boy some fun.

Nels ducked into the kitchen and grabbed the flashlight off the counter, where he kept it handy more for Homer than for potential blackouts.

Outside again, he stood in the backyard, switched on the flashlight and directed its beam to the grass, where it made a bright yellow circle. Homer froze in anticipation, ears up and tail wagging like a hummingbird's wings. Nels made the circle move and Homer screamed, literally screamed, with delight at this familiar and unendingly elusive prey. He chased the beam of light happily until he tired and then returned to sit as Nels's feet, tongue lolling out. Homer was an older guy, like Nels himself, and it took only a few minutes of play to wear him out.

Nels scratched him behind the ears. "You ready for bed, buddy?"

The dog hustled, best he could, through the kitchen door, which Nels held open for him. He followed behind, grabbing a dehydrated chicken treat from the pantry before heading off behind Homer toward the bedroom.

In the bedroom, Nels switched on the lamp. Homer was already on the bed, sprawled out, tail wagging, and eager for his usual bedtime treat. Nels tossed it to him.

After brushing his teeth and getting into a pair of cutoff sweats and a Pittsburgh Pirates T-shirt, Nels pulled back the covers and crawled into bed next to Homer. The dog curled up at his side as he'd done for so many years.

Nels thought he'd fall asleep as soon as his head hit the pillow, due to the three or four beers he'd had and being out so far beyond his usual bedtime of ten o'clock or so.

But he was wrong.

He couldn't stop thinking about Riccardo. About the miracle of fate, coincidences. About his grandson, being born today. About missed love and the possibilities he hoped to see come.

And about Cathy.

He thought that a quick text wouldn't hurt.

Call me in the morning. I have news.

He sent it and hoped it wouldn't wake her. But he did want her to see first thing when she did wake, so that maybe she could meet Riccardo before he headed back to New York, even if it meant the two of them racing to Pittsburgh International Airport in only a few hours.

He set the phone back down and snuggled beneath the sheet and quilt. Homer pawed at his chest to let him know to lift the quilt, so he could curl up beneath it, his own little cave.

Just as Nels's eyes were closing, the phone rang.

He rolled over and snatched the phone off the nightstand. It was Cathy.

"Hey! I'm sorry if I woke you."

Her voice, raspy, came through. "It's okay. I was up. Is everything okay?"

"Better than. I have news."

"Go on. Did you meet someone tonight? A special boy?" She laughed.

"Actually, I did." Nels shivered a bit as an unexpected chill coursed through him. "But it's not what you think." Nels sat up. The exhaustion he felt only moments before vanished and Nels didn't know where to look for it. He made sure Homer was comfortably burrowed under the cover and slipped silently out of the bedroom. As he walked, he talked. "I wish you'd stayed at the Q a little longer."

"Why's that?"

In the kitchen, Nels opened the fridge and grabbed his Brita pitcher and then poured himself a glass of water. He took a sip and answered. "You would have gotten the same surprise I did."

Cathy exhaled hard. "Look. It's late. Would you get to the point?"

Her curtness reminded him that it was indeed late, but also that he didn't really know her at all. "Sorry." He blurted out the whole tale about meeting Riccardo and who he was. It took fewer words and less time than Nels would have imagined. He ended with "And we have a grandson coming into the world in just a few hours."

He didn't know what to expect by way of response, but what he didn't expect was silence that dragged on and on until he said, "You're stunned, aren't you?"

"That's putting it mildly."

Nels was just about ready to launch into all the reasons she should be overjoyed, all the hope and prospective news these revelations promised, but before he could get even one word out, she said, "Listen, uh, I need to process this."

Her words hung in the air for a moment. He nodded and then realized she couldn't see him. "It's a lot to take in. Sorry. I get it. I just really meant to text you and then thought we'd talk in the morning."

"It's okay. I rarely sleep much, but I need to gnaw on this for a while."

"Aren't you happy?"

"I don't know, Nelson. It's a whole lot of shock. I'm gonna let you go."

Before she could hang up, Nels shouted, "Wait! I understand completely. My socks were knocked off too. I was thinking of maybe calling Riccardo in a few hours and see if I could give him a lift to the airport, or if he has a rental, meet up with him for coffee or even just a few minutes together. Would you like to come with me? Meet your son?" Why did Nels feel like he was on the losing end of an argument?

"Sure, Nelson. Sure. Why don't I come to your place in the morning?"

"Okay. That's not too far off! Make it early so we don't miss him. Six?"

"Sure. Gimme your address."

Nels did and then listened as the line went dead.

He stared for a while out the kitchen window and thought he saw the golden eyes of a fox looking back at him.

Chapter Twenty

My Lovely Man

Winslow sat, sobbing, among the grit and gravel.

He was in the driveway leading up to his house. In the dark, the blood appeared as dark stains on his T-shirt. He swore he could also feel it drying, crusty, on his skin.

Behind him, facedown, lay Chad. He wasn't moving.

A fingernail of moon looked down upon them, not judging, but simply observing. Lightning bugs danced in the air. Crickets sang. The wind rustled tree leaves. And the sky, once clear and starry, was beginning to cloud over, bringing the scent and promise of rain soon.

Heat lightning flashed in the distance, blue-white, followed by a growl of thunder.

"What have I done?" Winslow whispered to himself.

*

He'd left the Q an hour or so ago, on a high from his evening with Darryn. Their time together couldn't be classified as romantic, but it was hopeful. They sat next to each other on bar stools with their heads close together like conspirators. Their conversation had been a respite from Winslow's troubles with Chad, whom he hadn't talked about with Darryn. He hadn't even thought about him—and what a blessing *that* was. He and Darryn had actually laughed a lot, sharing life stories, aspirations, likes and dislikes. Darryn fast felt like an old friend. Winslow remembered, for the first time in a long while, what it was like to have a pal and to not feel so alone in the world.

After a couple of drinks, though, Darryn was getting light-headed and a little dizzy. This was a boy who hadn't had any experience at all with alcohol, even sweet shit like sloe gin, and it quickly showed.

"We should get you home."

"Are you propositioning me?" Darryn asked, slurring his words a tiny bit. He reached out and gently swiped a finger across Winslow's cheek.

"We should get you home—so you can sleep." Winslow thought it necessary to clarify.

They'd walked, arm in arm, out to the parking lot. The air was cooler and heat lightning illuminated the Appalachian foothills, transforming them into hulking dark beasts.

Had the light show been an omen?

The cooler air worked its magic immediately on Darryn. He paused for a moment, taking in the breeze, and then said, "Sorry. I was making a fool of myself back there."

"No. It was cute. We've all been there."

"Just getting this fresh air, I'm feeling a lot better now. And a little foolish."

"No worries. Still," Winslow said, "I should give you a lift home."

Darryn waved him away. "I'm okay to drive. Really. I wouldn't say that if it weren't true. I think everything just went to my head. Not only the booze, but you, the excitement of being out for the first time. Really, Winslow, I'm okay. And I don't want to put you out. It's not a long drive. You live around here so you also know there will be virtually no one on the road."

"Except for drunk drivers," Winslow added. "It's Saturday night in a place where there's little else to do other than get loaded."

"I know. I know. But really, Winslow, I'll be fine. My mama spies me pulling up with some dude, there's gonna be hell to pay."

"She doesn't know you're gay?"

"She doesn't know I'm male." He laughed. "Or that I grew up and somewhere along the way found a sex drive." Darryn leaned in as though to kiss Winslow, but Winslow knew in an instant he wasn't ready for that, pretty as Darryn was. He ducked back, pressing a hand to Darryn's chest.

"Sorry," Darryn muttered. "You're not into me."

"It's not that. You're adorable." He sighed and wondered if he should just tell him about Chad. But he was too tired, and that story was simply too long—and tragic. "I'm just worn out tonight."

He surprised himself by saying, "But I would like to see you again." *And in what world is that gonna work, Winslow? I'm sure Chad will be totally understanding, even if you're just friends.* Jealousy was one of Chad's ugliest attributes, and yet, Winslow had honestly never done a single deliberate thing to earn it. But, according to Chad, he was forever checking other guys out when they were in public. Old high school buddies he "friended" on Facebook were trying to steal him away. The pizza delivery guy was flirting. A call from a number that came up as unknown or private always prompted Chad to ask if it was his boyfriend calling. In Chad's world, paranoia reigned supreme.

"That would be wonderful, Mr. Birkel. Can we exchange numbers?"

Against his better judgment, he handed over his phone so Darryn could enter his number and Winslow did the same for him.

A little awkwardly, Winslow gave Darryn a one-armed hug and stepped back. "Now, you're sure you're okay to drive?"

"I'm fine, Ma." Darryn laughed. "Go. I'll call you tomorrow."

Terror leapt into his heart. "Not a good idea!" he snapped. And then tried to walk it back with a smile. "I, uh, probably won't be around a lot the next few days. I don't want to miss you. I'll call *you* real soon, okay?"

The disappointment on Darryn's face was plain. "Sure," he said.

"I will, really."

"Okay."

They stood in silence for a moment, and then Winslow turned to trudge back to his car. He gave Darryn a little wave over his shoulder but didn't look back. He imagined Darryn watching, smiling.

*

The rain began, soft patters at first, and then a hiss as drops descended on leaves and parched ground. Winslow raised his head, letting the warm water sluice over his face, erasing his tears.

And the blood.

He scooted back on his haunches, so he was alongside Chad, who still lay, unmoving, the gash in the back of his head still seeping, which the rain washed away for a moment; then the pool continued its growth—a black puddle.

"Chad?" Winslow put a hand to Chad's shoulder, shaking, as though Chad were taking a nap. In the gravel driveway. In the rain.

"Honey? I didn't mean it. I'm sorry. Please, please, please wake up. Oh god!"

The rain morphed quickly into a deluge, filling the air with its scent, soaking Winslow's clothes to his body. The temperature must have dropped fifteen, maybe even twenty degrees in the last ten minutes. Winslow shivered. His teeth chattered.

"Chad? Chad!" he cried louder, his call drowned out as the world went blinding white for a second; then a peal of thunder, ear-splitting, sounded. "Wake up," he whined. He placed his head on Chad's chest, listening, listening. "Don't do this to me."

He raised his head, certain the worst had happened—and it was, as Chad always accused, all Winslow's fault.

Winslow struggled to his feet and stood there, getting drenched. He raised his head and howled.

*

The car wouldn't start. Winslow had tried again and again to bring the Versa to life, but all he got when he turned the key in the ignition was a clicking sound. He knew he wasn't out of gas because he'd just filled the tank yesterday afternoon on his way home from work.

He tried again. Nothing. He lowered his head to the steering wheel in defeat. *This is where the evening turns ugly. This is where my little escape ends. This is when hell begins again, right where it left off.*

Wherever you go, there you are...

A knock on his driver's side window made him lift his head and look around, as though awakening.

Darryn stood outside the car, peering in.

Winslow tried to lower the window, but with no power, nothing happened. *Of course.* He motioned for Darryn to step back, which he did, and then Winslow slipped out of the car. "Piece of shit," he mumbled. He locked gazes with Darryn. "It's dead."

"Do you have triple A?" Darryn asked. "Jumper cables?"

"No and no."

Darryn smiled. "Then I guess it's me driving you home, instead of the other way around. Funny how life creates these opportunities out of shit circumstances. Good thing I sat in my car for a few, checking Twitter. I could have driven off, but no." He pulled his keyring out of his pocket and jingled them. "Here I am to save the day."

The prospect of Darryn driving Winslow home didn't relieve him, as it would any normal person. Instead, it filled him with dread bordering on horror.

"I can't let you do that," he snapped. He thought about how far he lived from the Q. Ten miles? Twelve? "I'll just walk. No prob."

"Don't be crazy. You're on my way."

Winslow went cold. He felt trapped. He couldn't have a guy driving him up to the house. No matter that the circumstances were completely innocent. The facts remained that Winslow had been out all Saturday night, at a gay bar, with a guy and that same guy was now driving him home. It would never fly. Winslow would be beaten within an inch of his life. The only luck he could pray for would be that he'd avoid any bones being broken or any lasting damage to his face.

It had happened before.

Why did he always go back? It was a good question and one for which Winslow simply didn't have an answer.

"I'm right over there." Darryn motioned to a little dark hatchback a few yards away. He pressed his key fob and the car beeped and the headlights flashed.

Winslow scratched at his neck. "I'll just call an Uber. I don't want to put you out. It's late." *Out here? I'll be lucky if a driver shows up before morning's light. And, if that happens, I'll be in even worse trouble.*

"I am driving you home." Darryn said it as though he really, really meant it and would accept no arguments.

Story of my life. I'm never in control. Reluctantly, he said, "Okay, but can you drop me at the end of my driveway? You don't have to take me up to the door. Promise me you won't take me to the front door."

Darryn cocked his head and his eyebrows moved toward each other, signaling his confusion. "Okay, if that's what it'll take."

They started toward Darryn's car, and Darryn asked, "I don't mean to pry, but is everything okay at home?"

"Peachy. Can we just go?"

Winslow followed Darryn to the car, his head hung low. Neither said another word.

*

"Right here. Drop me right here, okay?" Winslow pointed toward the mailbox at the end of their driveway.

"You sure?"

"Positive. Stop the car, please."

Darryn pulled over and they sat for a moment, listening to the engine idle. Thunder grumbled. "It's gonna rain soon, so I better scat," Winslow said, not looking at Darryn. He was afraid if he looked at him, he might talk. And if he talked, Darryn might—what? Want to protect him? Want to speak to Chad? Whisk him away from his troubles? All those options were laughable because they'd never happen.

He was trapped.

Darryn squeezed his shoulder, and the touch almost made him weep. Dread was a thing he could taste on his tongue, as though he'd sucked on a penny. He reached for the door handle.

Darryn asked, "Winslow? Are you *sure* you're okay?"

Before Winslow could wave away his concern or try to minimize it, Darryn went on. "We never talked about what I studied at school and what kind of job I'm looking for—social work. Buddy, I don't want to get all up in your business, but you seem like a person who's terrified to go back to his own house. It shouldn't be that way. Do me a favor and don't correct me again. I'm sensitive to things like this because of my own family. But that's a story for another time. But right now, just know I can take you anywhere you want to go. No questions asked."

The ball in Winslow's throat expanded, hurting. Tears ran down his cheeks. He let them fall for a moment, then wiped them away. He drew in a big breath. "I'm okay, Darryn. Really. You don't need to worry."

Darryn shook his head. "How 'bout we just talk? Either right here or you can call me later. You have my number now. Use it—anytime."

"I better go. Thanks for the lift." And before any more could be said, before his heart was broken by kindness and missed chances, he hopped from the car and slammed the door shut behind him in one quick, fluid motion. Darryn made no effort to move, so Winslow tapped on the trunk and shouted, "Thank you!"

Winslow watched the car disappear down the road with equal parts fear and longing.

He turned to trudge up the driveway and paused when he smelled cigarette smoke.

Chad emerged from behind a maple tree halfway up the driveway. Winslow assumed he'd stayed under the tree's canopy to protect his cigarette. He was wearing, without irony, a wifebeater, worn jeans, and work boots. He drew on his Marlboro Red and blew the smoke toward Winslow. The only expression on his face was a smirk. Winslow knew enough to know that the smirk was not even a distant relative to a smile. It was how Chad showed his disdain, his judgment, his loathing for Winslow, who had once again come up short in his estimation.

Winslow knew him well enough to understand that Chad needn't say a word. Winslow already knew the script by heart. Blood pounded a beat in his ears. His respiration quickened. He felt weirdly energized, but it wasn't a good feeling.

"Where have you been? I called your phone, texted you, over and over." He pulled his phone from his pocket, as though offering it to Winslow for proof.

"My battery was dying, so I shut it off."

Chad smiled broadly. "Of course you did. Why didn't I think of that?"

Winslow tried to hurry past him, and Chad grabbed his arm. His fingers dug hard into Winslow's bicep, making him wince in pain. "Now I have two questions." Chad took a final drag off his cigarette and flung it to the gravel. Winslow smelled whiskey seeping from his pores. This wasn't going to go well.

"Question number one, which you have yet to answer: Where the *hell* were you? And question number two: Where the hell do you think you're going?"

"I'm tired, Chad. Can't we just talk in the morning?" Chad didn't let go of his arm. In fact, he increased the pressure. It hurt. Winslow worried that the hand was a tourniquet, cutting off blood supply. He struggled to get free, but it was futile and only made Chad grip his arm tighter. Winslow made himself go limp, just a little, in hopes that it would reduce the pressure on his arm.

"It *is* morning, dumbass. So we can talk, yes?" Chad eyed him. The smile never left his face. Winslow had a fleeting thought: *How could one man be so beautiful on the outside and a monster within?*

Winslow hung his head. "Yes, Chad, we can talk. Could you let go of my arm though? It really hurts."

Surprisingly, Chad dropped his hand. Winslow took the opportunity, now free, to rush toward the house. *If I can make it to the door, I can lock it. And then maybe I can call Darryn.* Even as he thought the words, he recognized them for what they were—an empty and futile fantasy.

Chad was in quick pursuit. He was a big guy but fast.

It only took a second or two before Winslow felt himself tackled, dropping first to his knees, and ending with his face in the gravel. It burned as though it wasn't bits of stone beneath his cheek, but hot coals. He managed to wriggle free and scoot back on his butt. He touched his stinging chin, and his hand came away bloody.

Chad loomed above him.

Winslow eyed him, a whipped dog. "I, uh, just needed to get out. I took a drive and wound up down by the river." He didn't dare admit to Chad where he'd actually been. "I fell asleep in the car." The words sounded lame even to his own ears.

Chad took a few steps back. Winslow didn't dare rise. He stayed, cowed, sitting in the dirt and gravel. He was so drenched now that he didn't even notice the rain.

"Why do you have to insult my intelligence?"

"I'm not, Chad. I'm sorry." *Why am I even bothering? He's gonna beat me. I should just shut my pathetic loser mouth and take my medicine. Maybe if I don't argue too much, it won't be too bad. Maybe I'll be able to walk come morning light.*

"Yes. You are. Tell me where you were, Winslow. That guy who dropped you off? Did you suck his dick? Did he fuck your tight little ass?"

And then Chad was moving—fast. He grabbed Winslow's arm again and yanked him to his feet. "Let's see if he left a deposit." He was reaching for the button on Winslow's jeans, presumably to yank them down so he could shove a finger up his ass, testing for come. He'd done it before, even though he'd never found any evidence of infidelity on Winslow's part.

Winslow lurched away, trying to hold back the tears and the pleading words. "It wasn't like that! The Versa broke down. I think the battery died. He was just a good Samaritan who gave me a lift home. That's all."

Chad was silent. The rain dripping through the leaves seemed louder.

And then, like a bull, he lowered his head and charged toward Winslow. Winslow grunted as he slammed into his shoulder, hard, knocking him once again to the ground. He screamed as the back of his head hit the driveway. The wind knocked out of him, Winslow struggled to breathe. Finally, the breath rushed back into his lungs and he had trouble getting upright, even if it was only on his elbows.

His wind rushed out of him once again as Chad kicked him in the gut, hard, with the point of his work boot. Winslow saw stars and turned to his side as what little he'd eaten that day came up, tasting bitter and acidic.

"You pussy," Chad sneered and walked away, heading back toward the house.

Winslow sat up and watched him retreat. Things were far from over. If the scenario went according to script, he'd get up, nauseated, in tears, and would follow Chad back to the house. Once inside, Chad would interrogate him again. No matter what answer Winslow gave, Chad would believe nothing other than the lie that Winslow was off being unfaithful yet again.

Hopeless.

Winslow sat for a while, just letting the cool rain sluice over his face, providing scant comfort to his scrapes and cuts.

And then something happened inside—a switch from the script he'd followed the last few years with Chad. Something morphed—the same *something* that had changed earlier in the night when Winslow had dared to leave the house and go to the riverfront park and then the Q.

Maybe he *did* love himself a tiny bit. Perhaps, just this once in his young life, he was emboldened and came down on the side of fight instead of flee.

Literally, he saw red. The rage rose and enveloped him like a crimson cloud. He got to his feet, adrenaline pumping, and actually roared. He was beyond words.

Chad stopped. He turned in his tracks and laughed, really laughed, at Winslow charging toward him.

Maybe it was the lack of fear, the fact that Winslow was worthy only of his ridicule, that caught Chad off guard. Maybe he simply felt he had nothing left to lose.

Winslow ran into Chad like a bull into a red flag. Chad flew from his feet and Winslow would never forget, he was sure, the look of surprise on his face as he lost his balance. He tumbled backward. In a repeat of what he'd just inflicted on Winslow, he hit his head hard on the ground below.

Blood seeped quickly from the back of his head and even a small trickle from his right ear. He grunted and his eyes fluttered closed.

That's when Winslow squatted down beside him, begging him to respond.

But there was nothing. Winslow leaned in finally, close, and listened for Chad's breath. Thank God, it was there.

Winslow stood once more. He felt a paradoxical mix of terror, nausea, and freedom.

The rain slowed. A car swept by on the road, not slowing, its tires hissing on the slick pavement.

Winslow turned and began walking back down the driveway. He kept glancing over his shoulder, expecting Chad to rise up, like Michael Myers at the end of *Halloween*, and pursue him.

Yet Chad lay still.

Oh god, please don't let me have killed him. He didn't believe he could have because he didn't honestly know what it would take to eradicate such evil and cruelty.

At the end of the driveway, Winslow breathed in deep. His side ached, and he wondered if Chad had cracked a rib or two—again—when he kicked him. He wondered if he was bleeding internally.

The rain ceased coming down as suddenly as it had begun.

The one thing he had lied about to Chad was his phone. It wasn't out of charge. He woke it and made two calls—the first to 911, where he requested an ambulance for an injured man. The second was to Darryn, who answered after just a single ring, even though he sounded sleepy.

"Come and get me, please," Winslow said. "I'll be walking down the road. Hurry." And then he hung up.

And he began his journey away from the man who'd made his life a living hell. He had the clothes on his back, his phone, keys on a ring, and a wallet with a couple credit cards, an insurance card, a frequent shopping card for a local grocer's, and twenty-six dollars in cash.

Winslow didn't know what would happen next, but anything was preferable to this excuse of a life he'd allowed himself to endure.

An unrecognizable fluttering in his gut caused him to pause, wondering what the sensation could be.

Happiness, maybe? Hope?

Part Four

There's Got to Be a Morning After

Chapter Twenty-One

It's Too Late

Wally sat on the patio out back with a cup of tea. Steam rose from the reddish liquid before being snatched away by the breeze. It was just before sunrise, when the sky takes on a gray hue, infused with a mysterious light source. The air was damp. When the wind blew, it had an undercurrent of chill.

It had stopped raining a while ago and now there were no clouds. Droplets still slid off leaves and glistened in the grass. The moon was pale, translucent, high up. Next to it, Venus shone brightly, more than a star.

He sipped his tea, feeling nothing. He knew he should be enraged, or worried, or crying, but he felt absolutely zilch, as though his well of emotions had run dry.

Joel wasn't home yet. Wally had searched for him again and again throughout the night, but never saw him after they parted ways early in the evening. The bartender, Mary Louise, had gone above and beyond with her kindness, perhaps sensing Wally's distress as anyone in her position (someone with a fingertip on the pulse of human emotion) might. She'd slipped free drinks in front of him, cracked corny jokes, and made it a point to linger nearby when her work allowed, just chatting.

He knew what she was up to. She was trying, as most bartenders do, to make him forget. Bartenders didn't deal in alcohol or currency. They dealt in oblivion.

But he couldn't forget Joel had abandoned him at this little rural bar. Wally had searched the dance floor, the room with the video games and the pool table, the parking lot, and even the men's room. Joel had become an elusive phantom. Wally imagined, with each search, he'd just missed him. In his more paranoid moments, he thought not only that he'd just missed his husband, but that Joel had seen him and was hiding.

When the evening wore down to nothing and the music stopped, Wally had to accept Joel wasn't going to turn up to flirt with him as though they'd just met. Somewhere, their plan of earlier had gone awry, slipping out of Wally's control. Wally had sat, shoulders hunched, at the bar, watching as the crowd of revelers dwindled. When the lights came on, they revealed the bar for the sad and decrepit locale it was—darkness had given it magic.

Wally was alone.

Mary Louise approached him, and Wally almost burst into tears at the expression she failed to hide—more than sympathy—it was pity.

"He didn't turn up?"

"Can one be stood up or I guess the better term would be *ditched* by one's own husband?" Wally asked.

"Well, I think you already know the answer to that, my friend. Listen, we need to close up now. I wish I could let you hang out while I close, but you can't be in here. I did, though, want to be sure you were okay and that you had a way home."

Wally bit his lower lip, knowing her kindness could easily make him cry, and he didn't want to appear weak in front of this generous woman. He had, in fact, checked the parking lot for the car only fifteen minutes ago, and it had still been there.

"I'm okay. The car's in the parking lot. Wish I could say the same for Joel." He laughed, but Mary Louise didn't join him. She reached out and placed her hand over his. She left them joined like that for a moment, then squeezed his hand before letting go.

"I'll be done here in about a half hour, maybe even less, if you want to wait for me."

"Why would I do that?" Wally asked, then regretted sounding harsh. "I appreciate your concern. I really do. But I'm a grown man, and I think I can take care of myself."

"I don't doubt it a bit. I hope you get home and figure out a reasonable explanation for your hubby's whereabouts."

"Oh, there's a reasonable explanation," Wally said. "I just don't know how much I like it."

Mary Louise nodded. "Well—"

Wally cut her off, holding up a hand. "I know. I know. You need me out of here."

"If I could, I'd let you stay."

"I know. You've been so nice tonight, way more than you needed to be, making me feel cared about. Don't think I didn't notice, and don't believe, for one second, that I don't appreciate it. Because I do. Most of us these days are so absorbed in our own dramas that we fail to notice someone else's pain."

As Wally uttered the words, he realized how much he was hurting.

He'd slid off the stool and walked out, waving to Mary Louise over his shoulder. He knew he'd most likely never see her again.

And now, he stood on his own back patio. The quiet of the dawn breaking kept him company. He awaited the sun's rise and Joel's return home.

Where is he?

Who's he with?

Has something bad happened?

Define bad.

Wally drained the tea from the cup and closed his eyes, closing down his worried mind at the same time. He didn't want to think, to torment himself, most of all with conclusions his cunning subconscious had already drawn.

He cocked his head as he heard the grumble of a car engine in the distance. It slowed and then stopped, engine idling.

Joel was coming home.

But was this even home anymore?

He waited, hands at his sides. The sky morphed from a purplish pale light to a golden, warmer illumination.

And there he was—his beautiful man—Joel.

They faced each another across the fieldstone pavers. Joel looked frightened, cowed.

The sky continued its reliable progress toward another day.

Joel spoke first. "I'm sorry." He held out his hands, palms upraised, plaintive. "What happened wasn't what I intended."

Wally blurted, "How did you get home?" There were so many things he wanted to ask. He surprised himself this was first. But he really wanted to know and realized what Joel would say next could be revelatory.

"A friend. A friend gave me a ride." Joel snorted and corrected himself. "Gave me a lift." He regarded Wally with scared, sad eyes, like a dog afraid he was about to be bopped on the nose with a rolled-up newspaper.

Now, Wally realized, there was no room for denial, for misunderstanding. Deep down inside, he'd wanted this to be over, even if the desire wasn't at the forefront of his consciousness. Where their marriage would go after this conversation, he wasn't sure. It wouldn't be back to a normal that had perhaps never existed, or at least not in recent memory. Even though Wally was weary to his very bones, he needed to talk to Joel, really talk. "Just to be clear—you cheated on me tonight, right? I don't want, can't bear, details, I just need a yes or no. And please—we're beyond subterfuge right now, so don't insult my intelligence."

Joel looked down at the ground, rubbing the toe of his shoe against the fieldstone. After a moment, he lifted his head and met Wally's gaze. "Yes."

There was a lurch in Wally's gut. Until the yes was uttered, hope lived, however irrational. For a fleeting moment, he struggled to keep down the food he'd consumed that day. After a couple deep breaths, the nausea passed. "Thank you. Not for cheating, of course, but for not trying to deny it." *What do I say now? What do I do?* Wally plopped down in the chair behind him, knees weak.

Joel sat across. "I never meant for things to get so out of hand. I was a little drunk and..." his voice trailed off.

"One thing led to another?" Wally shrugged. "I told you. I don't want details." He considered asking Joel what they should do now. Did he want to stay together? Did they need to go to counseling? But then, he had an epiphany—he knew what to do now, and *he* needed no counseling.

"What *do* you want?" Joel asked.

"I can tell you what I *don't* want. I guess that's a start. I don't want to hear you say you made a mistake. I don't want to hear that it didn't *mean anything*. Because if you're willing to risk our thirty years together over something that meant nothing, then I'd be offended." Wally wondered where his rage was, where the tears were, why he felt so numb.

What Wally did understand, though, was that he didn't want to talk things out. He didn't want an explanation. He didn't want to go inside and crawl into bed with this man with whom he'd shared his life for three decades.

It was over.

It was that simple. In a way, it was a relief.

He'd thought for so many years that Joel was too good for him because of his charm, his good looks, and his vitality. But the truth was, Wally now realized, that it was *he* who was too good for Joel. Wally's qualities weren't as flashy as Joel's—trustworthiness, kindness, compassion, fidelity—but they were more valuable.

And maybe he was grateful to Joel for making things so clear-cut. It was as though a switch had been flipped. The switch was *not* a toggle. Once flipped, it stayed put.

"You know, I fought all my life trying to be accepted. First, for just being who I was. And then by pretty men, for whom I seemed to be invisible. I was always grateful that you saw me. But maybe you didn't. Maybe you saw only your own reflection when you looked in my eyes. Maybe not. Maybe you just stopped seeing me over the course of years. Whatever the reason, last night was my cue. I'm not gonna ignore it.

"Was it Madonna who sang about not standing for second best? That we'd do better on our own?" Wally chuckled. "You're the fan. You know better than I would. But I do share the sentiment.

"And you know what? I realize something, right here, right now." Wally paused for a moment. "I like being alone. Maybe I always have."

Wally debated if he should confess what he'd thought through all the years together, a secret buried so deep he could barely acknowledge it even to himself.

He had nothing to lose. "I had this little fantasy. Not the kind you have. But about me. I always imagined that someday you'd be gone, and I'd be on my own. I'd have my own little place, a dog or a cat, and a few good friends. But I'd glory in mornings like this one, making my tea, putting on some classical music, reading a good book. Not having to answer to anyone. Not having to try to please…

"See, I went along with your little plan last night—your effort to spice things up—because I wanted to please you. I didn't want to. And in my passive-aggressive way, I showed you that. But you didn't want to see. You could only see what you wanted.

"Sweetheart, it's been a good ride, a long ride, and make no mistake—I will take many happy memories from our time together." Wally looked around, almost surprised that the sun had come up fully and the birds were singing. The automatic sprinklers came to life in their yard. "But we're done."

Wally tried to think of something more to say, but there really wasn't anything. He didn't dare look at Joel, so he simply got up and ambled toward the house. He walked slowly, listening for a word, a call to come back, to talk more.

When he heard only birdsong, he went into the house, where he could begin packing a bag.

Chapter Twenty-Two

If I Could

Nels set the phone on the kitchen table, next to a plate of toast crumbs and a half cup of coffee, gone tepid. It was past the time he'd wanted to go to Riccardo's motel, but he'd hoped Cathy Corak would be at his side. Hadn't she agreed to show up this morning at his house?

He'd called, texted, repeated the process again and again, imagining her phone's battery had died, or that the device was in another room, or that she was sleeping.

But he knew the truth when it stared him in the face.

Cathy didn't want to join him this morning. Nels was old enough and wise enough to realize he shouldn't try to ascribe motivation to her silence and her absence. He could be angry at her for turning away from this chance at meeting not only her son, but maybe even her grandson. He could be sad for her for being unable to do those things.

In the end, he knew not to take her refusal to show up to talk this morning personally. He didn't really know her, despite the huge role she'd played, albeit unwittingly, in his life. Too many years apart. And the small glimpse she'd given him the night before showed him a life that perhaps had been eroded by too many bad choices. He could speculate that the beginning of the wrong turns began when she became pregnant by him. But then who really knew what someone else's motivations were?

He called to Homer and put on his leash and harness. The old boy would water a couple bushes in the front yard and then would want to come back in for his kibble. There'd been a time when the dog would love the morning and would walk for a good half hour or more, glorying in the scents of early morning.

Once he'd fed Homer, he headed back outside.

In the car, he fastened his seat belt, put NPR on the radio, and headed out to the little motel where Riccardo had told him he was staying.

*

When the door opened, Nels was relieved to see the look of pleased surprise on Riccardo's face. "You came? I wasn't sure." He peered around Nels so he could look out into the parking lot.

"She's not with me. I'm so sorry." Nels considered offering an excuse but decided it wasn't his place. What Cathy Corak might want from this young man, or not, was truly up to her. He was linked with the woman in a profound but oddly superficial way. Whatever future this

Riccardo might have with his biological mother was now between them.

"Can I come in?" Nels asked.

"Sure, sure." Riccardo stepped back, and Nels stepped into a motel room that could have been anywhere in America—bland landscapes on the wall, worn carpeting, vinyl laminate furniture, the obligatory ice bucket and the drinking glasses with their paper caps. Riccardo's bed was made and that fact caused a smile to rise to Nels's lips. He didn't say it aloud, but his thought was, *Like father like son.*

"Any news?"

"Oh yeah," Riccardo responded. "There's news all right." And his face lit up with joyous illumination. "My son, and your grandson, Tate, arrived just over an hour ago." As though delivering the news was too much for him, Riccardo plopped down on the edge of the bed, a little out of breath. He shook his head. "I missed the birth, unfortunately. But I couldn't be happier. I'm a dad!"

Nels experienced a strange stirring that made him want to laugh and cry at the same time. How much he'd lost! How much he might gain!

The world was forever changed.

"That's wonderful." Nels kept a discreet distance as he sat next to his son. They were quiet for a moment, the bright sun illuminating dust motes.

Riccardo stood and snatched his phone off the round table near the window. "Wanna see some pics?"

"Of course!" Nels leaned in—and there he was, his grandson, Tate. Just twenty-four hours ago, he didn't even know he had a son, and now the world, fate, whatever, had delivered to him a son *and* a grandson. Nels had lived long enough to know that the one thing you could take to the bank about life was its unpredictability.

The baby, swaddled in a fleecy-looking blue-striped blanket and wearing a tiny red knit beanie on his head, looked like all other babies. Squinched-up slits for eyes, flaky pink skin that was almost opalescent, so new, so untouched. Impossibly tiny fingers reached toward the camera.

Riccardo swiped again and the new pic revealed mother and son in a hospital bed. "Maya's beautiful," Nels said softly. And she really was, despite looking completely exhausted, but she reminded him a bit of the actress, Halle Berry. She had the same cheekbones, the same perfect teeth and flawless skin. Her hair was cropped short and, even though there wasn't a spot of makeup anywhere in view, she was stunning, with wide green eyes flecked with gold.

"I got very lucky," Riccardo said. "Why she settled for a schlub like me, I'll never know." He chuckled.

Nels playfully punched his upper arm. "Don't sell yourself short. You're a handsome man." It had been on his lips to say, "Just like your old man," but he didn't think he had the right.

Not yet.

"I can't wait to get home to them. This feels like a dream. I can't even believe it."

"I'll bet. Tate looks healthy and sweet. And your love for him is already there. You're going to be a wonderful father."

"I know I should be happy he's those things, and I am, but between you and me, I'm so thrilled to have a little boy."

Nels grinned and eyed Riccardo. "Me too," he said in a voice he thought was just beneath audible.

But Riccardo heard and leaned over to give Nels a quick hug.

He leapt from the bed. "My flight leaves in a couple hours, so I better be heading out. I'm one of those people who likes to get to the airport super early, just in case."

"I'm the same way," Nels said.

Riccardo nodded and they sat together in companionable silence for a moment or two more, shoulders touching and, Nels suspected, thoughts aligned on new beginnings. Nels didn't know what more to say and suspected that Riccardo didn't either. Sure, there was a lot to be voiced and a lot of words, histories, stories, hopes and dreams needed to be exchanged. But that would come with time—and time was the one thing Nels worried was running short.

"How I wished I had known you from the start!" he cried, thinking of all the years and years that had gone by, all he had missed.

"I wish that too. I loved my parents dearly, but it would have been nice to have you in my life as well. All we can do now is move forward." Riccardo closed and zipped shut his suitcase, set it on end, and pulled out the retractable handle. "This is just our beginning."

How Nels longed to hear him add, *Dad*, to the end of that sentence.

Patience. You gotta have patience.

Nels stood and followed Riccardo to the door. "You all checked out?"

"Yup."

They stood for a moment, awkward as two strangers, which they essentially were. But Nels's DNA, his blood flowed through this man. That was a bond, wasn't it?

Nels wanted to ask so many things:

Would you consider calling me dad?

Do you think with time and good behavior, you'll come to love me as much as I already love you?

Do you think there'll be a place for me in your life?

Where do we go from here?

When can I see you again?

When can I see the baby, meet Maya?

He wanted to ask all these things and, yet, knew he shouldn't. This wasn't a Hallmark movie. This wasn't a happy-ever-after fairy tale. This was real life. Nels would have to be patient, letting Riccardo and his family come to him on their own terms, in their own times. If there was a place for Nels in this new family, he knew it couldn't be achieved by force or longing.

Riccardo opened the door and stood there, silhouetted by the bright sun outside, waiting for Nels. He followed Riccardo out of the room and walked over to a red compact car, his rental. It beeped as he unlocked the door and the trunk popped open. Riccardo placed his bag inside and then turned to Nels.

He hugged Nels, but it was awkward, and Nels stepped back quickly. He felt a ball forming in his throat, painful, but he managed a smile. "Safe travels." He bit off saying, *son*. Instead, he simply repeated, "Safe travels."

"Thanks." Riccardo smiled and, oddly enough, Nels saw not himself in the smile, but his own father. He got into the car and slammed the door. He started the engine.

Nels waited, hand at the ready to wave as he drove away.

But Riccardo lowered the window. "Once we get settled back in the city, I hope you'll come see us. Meet Maya and little Tate."

Nels bit back the tears. He was so grateful that he, right then and there, committed this precious invitation to memory. "Of course. I'd love that." And then, even though he knew it was foolish and sentimental, he told Riccardo he loved him.

Riccardo stared at him for a moment and then said, quickly, "I love you too."

And then he drove away, and Nels waved and waved.

Chapter Twenty-Three

Dreamweaver

Gracie stood in the doorway of Rose's room, watching her sleep. Her eyes filled with tears of gratitude and, yes, adoration. Asleep, there was something childlike about Rose, wiping years off her face. There was the young girl she'd fallen in love with all those years ago and never had the courage to profess it.

She crept closer and spotted movement beneath Rose's eyelids, back and forth, back and forth. *What's she dreaming of? Do I dare hope in my parched heart it's me? Or is it a nightmare, reliving the moment of the crash's impact?* As much as Gracie wanted it, entrance to Rose's dream world would always be barred, no matter how things worked out from this moment forward. Dreams were perhaps the one thing we could all claim as belonging to ourselves exclusively.

An ugly purple bruise ran along Rose's left cheekbone and her arm was in a sling. There was a big uncomfortable-looking collar around her neck. Still, she was lovely. Rose was always lovely—as sweet and beautiful as the flower for which she was named. Her blonde hair lay against the pillow, and Gracie wanted nothing more than to run her fingers through the silky multicolored strands. She closed her eyes for a moment, feeling the silk of it beneath her fingertips.

Rose let out a muffled sigh and rolled over on her side. She was deep under and that was a good thing, Gracie supposed. Rose needed rest to heal and recover. Gracie sat in the blue vinyl guest chair next to the bed and let her head recline for a moment on its back. She would remain here throughout the night and for as long as Rose needed her.

She'd actually begun to drift off a bit when she heard her name. Her eyelids fluttered.

"Gracie?" Rose repeated, voice groggy and clouded with sleep.

Gracie stood. She hesitated for a moment but then allowed herself to go with instinct. She clutched Rose's hand in her own. Rose flesh was soft, hot. Gracie hoped she'd never have to let go. With her other hand, she stroked Rose's forehead for a moment and smiled down. "How you feeling?"

Rose let out a sigh. "My head hurts. My ribs hurt. I feel like I've been through the wringer." Rose made a valiant attempt to smile but didn't really succeed. Still, it was wonderful to witness her try.

"I'm sure. You've been through a lot. You remember what happened?"

"Every minute. I wish I didn't, but the crash keeps replaying in my head, even when I don't want it to. My only way out is sleep."

"That's common with trauma. Are you on something for pain?"

"Vicodin, yup. It's a real treat," Rose laughed, but then groaned. "But not enough of one." She slumped down into the pillow more, eyebrows furrowed together.

Gracie smoothed away some hair from her forehead. "You should rest. I'll go see if the nurse is around—maybe they can give you another, uh, treat."

Gracie turned to exit the room, but Rose called her back.

Rose pointed to the drawn curtain separating her from the other bed in the room. It was dark and still over there. When Gracie had come into the room, she'd seen an old woman, with coarse gray hair and a wizened face, sleeping. Rose whispered, "Is Liz over there?"

Gracie's heart broke a little. She shook her head. "No, sweetie, no. She's, uh, down the hall. They're looking after her." She couldn't bear to tell Rose the truth, not now. There would be plenty of time to approach Liz's demise in the morning. There was nothing anyone could do.

"That's good. I'm glad they're taking care of her. I was worried." Rose snuggled down under the thin blanket. "I think I'm due for another treat, Gracie, so you go ahead and work your magic."

Gracie didn't know if she really *did* need another Vicodin because Rose's eyelids were struggling to stay up. Pausing near the doorway, Gracie watched her beloved for a moment. A moment was all it took for her to fall asleep again.

Gracie tiptoed back to her chair and sat, waiting.

She remained there until dawn's washed-out light woke her. All was silent on the floor at this early hour. Gracie glanced over at Rose and was surprised to see she was awake and watching her. Her eyes were brighter. She seemed a little more alive than she had yesterday, a bit more coherent and aware.

"Did you know you drool when you sleep? And you snore like a truck driver."

Gracie chuckled. "Been watching me for a while, huh?" She stood so she could stand beside the bed and hold Rose's hand. "How would you know how a truck driver sounds?"

"Oh, you'd be surprised at what I know." Rose's blue eyes searched Gracie's own. Gracie couldn't help it—she reached down and kissed her forehead. Could she say the words she'd come here to say? Could she confess? Would it be good for her soul?

Gracie wanted to kiss Rose on the lips, desperately. But she knew her night spent asleep in the guest chair would have surely left her with a monstrous case of morning mouth. And besides, would Rose welcome it? Or would she shove her away, affronted?

Stop it! Just stop second-guessing yourself. You'll never get anywhere with her if you continue with the defeatist thinking even before you start. Honestly, you're your own worst enemy.

"Rose? How are you feeling?"

"Hungry."

Gracie laughed. It was a long-standing joke that Rose could eat whatever she liked and as much of it without ever gaining an ounce. Liz had called Rose "hollow leg." Sure, she was a little thicker than she was when they'd first met, but she still had curves that commanded attention.

"I'm sure they'll bring you something soon." Gracie glanced over at the clock on the wall and saw that it was only a little after six.

"Yeah, some crappy powdered scrambled eggs or a bowl of blah oatmeal."

"Would you like me to go to Maxie's and get you breakfast? I can. It'll take me a half hour or so." Maxie's was an old-school diner a couple of blocks from the hospital. They made no concessions to healthy eating, but their hash browns were the best in town, and their Western omelet was to die for. The biscuits and gravy were artery-clogging heaven.

"Oh, would you, Gracie? Please! That would be great." Rose sat up straighter in the bed, using the remote to bring the bed up to support her back. The prospect of a full Maxie's breakfast seemed to make her even more vital.

"Of course, I would. What would you like?"

"I trust you. Surprise me."

Gracie nodded, smiling, and thinking how much she loved this woman. She'd buy out Maxie's for her and stop at L&B Donuts, too, just for good measure. She started out of the room but then turned back, feeling as though she were being propelled by outside forces.

"You really want me to surprise you?" Gracie came back and sat on the edge of the bed. This was a now or never moment. "Do you think I still can, after all these years?"

"Yeah, sure."

Gracie leaned in close to Rose and said, "I love you."

Rose grinned. "I love you, too, Gracie. I always have. You're the best friend a gal could ask for."

Gracie sighed. "Okay. I need to clarify, sweetie. I love you as in I'm *in* love with you. I love you like Corky loved Violet in *Bound*, like Idgie loved Ruth in *Fried Green Tomatoes*. I love you with all my heart, and I think I have ever since I first laid eyes on you, way back in the day."

There. It's out. Let the chips fall where they may.

Rose stared at Gracie in stunned silence, mouth hanging open. She said nothing for such a long time that Gracie began to wish she'd held her feelings inside, as she was accustomed to doing. *Now you've done it. Made an ass of yourself. And probably, you blew up any chance at friendship too.* Before Rose could try to make her feel better with some pathetic platitude, Gracie said, "I better go get you that breakfast."

She started to get off the bed, but Rose pulled her back. "Really, Gracie? Really?"

Their gazes locked and Gracie said, softly, "Yes, really. Cat's out of the bag now." She laughed self-consciously.

"Why didn't you ever tell me?"

"I don't know." Gracie shrugged. "Didn't want to bust up the trio, I guess."

"Oh, honey, you could never do that."

And Gracie thought of poor Liz, somewhere nearby, hovering between life and death. Before the day was over, she'd be gone and the trio would be "busted up" anyway. Beyond her control.

Rose swallowed. "When I said I love you, I meant it." She smiled, "I meant it in the same way you do." Rose's smile was as sweet as ever. "Will you hold me?"

Gracie, usually stoic, felt the tears spring from her eyes. She gathered Rose in her arms and pulled her close.

"Ouch! Goddamn you! Watch my arm!"

Gracie pulled back, laughing. "Oh, I'm so sorry!" She started to stand.

"Get back here," Rose said. "Just be careful, okay?"

This time, Gracie *gingerly* enveloped Rose in a hug. Rose whispered, "I wish you would have told me sooner."

"I wish I would have too. But I was afraid."

"Of what?"

"Getting hurt, getting rejected."

Rose shushed her. "That's the risk we take. But it's okay. You're here now, and we know our feelings now. This is day one for us."

Gracie started to get up again. She still had her fool's mind on food.

"No." Rose threw back the covers. "Get in with me. We'll snuggle here together until some homophobic nurse wags a finger and tells us we can't do that."

"What about your breakfast?"

"They'll bring me some food. Don't worry about it."

And Rose lay close to Gracie, her hair and skin mingling with Gracie's, under the worn blue blanket. Rose slept. And Gracie lay awake, unsure if she was in a hospital...or heaven.

When Gracie closed her own eyes and drifted off, she dreamt of the three of them dancing together at the Q. When the fast music changed tempo, morphing into a song Gracie had always loved, Etta James crooning "At Last," Liz pushed Rose toward Gracie, urging them to dance.

Over Rose's shoulder, Gracie watched Liz retreat, walking farther and farther away until the shadows consumed her.

Epilogue

Mary Louise sat alone on her back porch. Before her were the remains of what she called breakfast: an empty coffee cup and an ashtray full of butts. Not pretty, but necessary to revive her in the morning these days. The sun had crept up over the tree-covered hilltops and warmed her face. Cicadas sang in the branches of the big maple near her house.

Her laptop was open on the redwood-stained picnic table. She'd searched for news about the accident last night but was unable to find anything she didn't already know. In a little while, she'd call Billy or the hospital to see what was what and if there was anything she could do to help. She'd prayed this morning, and before falling into bed earlier, that Rose and Liz would survive and thrive. And the act revealed Mary Louise's deep concern. She rarely, if ever, prayed.

The people at the Q were her children, in a way. Whether their acquaintance was one of many years or they'd just met one night and then never showed again, she cared about each and every one who wandered into the bar. She served up more than drinks. She served love and compassion. She served concern because she genuinely loved every person who came in and bellied up to her bar. Their dreams, their hopes, their squabbles and celebrations were all hers too. When she was back in Chicago, years ago, she'd never dreamed she'd be riding out these twilight years in her hometown, tending bar and fixated on all her patrons in a motherly way. If you'd even suggested such a thing to her back in the days when she was a fixture at bars like Sidetrack and Roscoe's, she would have laughed you out of the room.

And yet, here she was. Mama Mary Louise, keeping watch over her charges.

The laptop was out for a reason beyond checking the news. Mary Louise had long thought she should write about her experiences at the bar, how the stories she witnessed every night she worked there reflected not just their owners' joys and despairs but also how they reflected *everyone's*. The bar was a microcosm. Sure, it was small town Appalachia, but the human drives behind the drinking, dancing, and flirting were all the same, whether you were in Chicago, New York, London, Paris, or Hong Kong.

She'd begun writing a bit about herself and how she'd come to this point in her life, and then she highlighted all she'd written and hit delete. It wasn't right. Sure, she'd be part of the story, but as an observer, not a central character. She'd be freer to talk about the beginnings and endings that transpired every night the bar was open.

Funny, Mary Louise mused, as a profound thought occurred to her. *All the endings are really beginnings and vice versa.* That's just how life went. When Mary Louise moved back to Hopewell, she thought it was the end of her life, the end to her dreams of having someone to love. She thought she'd failed, slogging home with her shoulders hunched and her tail between her legs, beaten by life. But now, she had the wisdom to see that things had worked out just as she supposed they should have—and, she was happy here, alone, on this back porch with birds singing and the sun promising a hot and humid day.

Anything was possible.

Anything she chose to make happen.

She brought up her Word document and began writing:

First, no one ever called it the Quench Room. To its patrons, it was just the Q. Many of them weren't even aware of its proper name.

She tapped her lips with her finger, what should come next? Would the words flow freely, or would she have to yank them out forcefully, each one a battle?

The phone rang and she looked down at its screen. Billy Breedlove was calling. Odd for him to call this early, odd for him to call at all, really. Like almost all of her friendships, they came to life when she entered the bar and ended when she walked out.

Maybe that was about to change. Maybe Billy realized she had a little crush and was calling to ask her to take a drive, perhaps over to Mill Creek Park near Youngstown. They'd go later for hamburgers and ice cream.

Stop being silly.

"Hey." Mary Louise said after pressing Accept.

"Hey yourself." Billy's voice was gruff and it gave Mary Louise a little shiver. "I'm just calling because I have news."

"The accident?"

"Yeah. I know you already heard. But I can confirm that Liz is gone. Of course, not yet, technically, but they're pulling the plug later."

Mary Louise sucked in a breath. A tear dribbled down her cheek. An image came to mind—Liz dancing all by herself in the center of the dance floor, swirling to a song by Mary Chapin Carpenter, "I Take My Chances."

Fitting.

Mary Louise pressed a hand to her eyes and tried to rein in the sobs she knew were coming. She thought of the line in the song about never learning anything from playing it safe, and it gave her an idea.

"I'm so sorry," Mary Louise said when she could speak. "Is she still in a coma like Gracie said.?"

"Yeah. I heard she was brought in that way. They haven't been able to revive her."

"A shame. She was spunky, that one."

Billy chuckled. "That's for sure. Hell of a pool player too."

Mary Louise wasn't surprised when their chatter quieted. Billy was never much of a talker. She drew in a shaky breath and noticed how the leaves whispered to one another. Reminding herself of taking chances, she plunged in. "Since we're both off tonight, how about you and me celebrate Liz's life together? I'll make us a little supper. I got some salmon in the fridge and can bake a couple potatoes, throw together a salad. Pour us a glass of wine. We can toast to her memory."

Billy was silent for so long Mary Louise began to think he was appalled. She wanted to rush in and remind him that she understood he was celibate and that this wasn't a date, but then he spoke.

"That would be nice. Can I bring dessert?"

Mary Louise barked out a delighted laugh. "Yes, you can. As long as it's not something made by Hostess. Mary Louise doesn't do Twinkies."

That got a laugh from him. "I was thinking a lemon meringue pie."

"Bricker's, across the river, makes good ones."

"I make my own. Better."

"I'll be the judge of that. Six?"

"Okay." And he hung up.

Beginnings. Endings.

I always imagined him as a little boy, my little boy. A tow-headed rascal—he couldn't be contained. Forever into something. Breaking things. Ruining things. Making a mess. But it was okay, because he was mine. It was okay because he was so damn cute. I imagine him growing into a young boy, all gangly arms and scraped knees. A teenager—sullen and unresponsive, not wanting to be seen with me, but oh my, how vulnerable, how fragile and easily hurt. I can see him as a young man, strapping, blond, towering over me. But always a mama's boy...

Smiling, Mary Louise returned to her keyboard.

And many, gay, straight, and otherwise inclined, imagined the Q stood for Queer. Some saw it as an affirming name: and some whispered it, snickering.

Second, unless you knew what you were looking for, you'd drive right by the Q, not thinking its sad, nondescript exterior housed much of anything. The Q, located on a two-lane country road just outside the small town of Hopewell, West Virginia was in a squat, gray cinder block building. It had no front door—patrons entered through a chipped red-painted door off the gravel parking lot in the back. Out front, there was no sign—neon or otherwise—proclaiming the Quench Room or even the Q. The single window out front, long and rectangular, was black tinted so passersby couldn't see inside.

The Q's nearest neighbors were an auto-body shop called, charmingly, Gomer's, and, down the road just a bit, a no-name bait and tackle shop, open only in summers, for those fishing on the mighty Ohio River, just a couple miles away.

The Q didn't look like a place where people celebrated.

It didn't appear to be an establishment where people hooked up, hoping for a raunchy one-night stand or dreaming of a lifetime commitment—and everything in-between. A casual glance would never inspire the idea that the Q was a place for socializing, dancing, and drinking.

Mary Louise closed her eyes for a moment. She tilted her head back, luxuriating in the sun warming her face.

After a moment, she opened her eyes again, sat up straighter, placed her hands on the keys, and returned to writing her story. Their story. All of their stories.

Acknowledgements

This is a story of the heart. My heart. I grew up in an area very much like the little area you read about here and, in those Appalachian foothills, my roots remain. Although, as young boy and man, I wanted nothing more than to leave behind that twisty murky river and those tree-covered hills, they stubbornly stay strong within me.

I dedicated the book to my little sister (she's not so little now, with two grown children), Melissa, and I want to say thank you to her for bringing me out one Saturday night when I was back home, visiting. I went with her and her husband Vince to the race track and casino, Mountaineer, across the Ohio River in West Virginia. It was a familiar haunt for Melissa and her husband, Vince. Of course I, ever the introvert, didn't want to go, but I'm so glad I did because that night inspiration for this book was born.

As a writer, I never know from where an idea will come. But that night, at Mountaineer, dancing and drinking with Melissa and her friends—a crew of regulars for whom this was a weekly highlight—I realized I wanted to write about these people. Not gay people, but small town people who come together as a community in a shared space. People who let off the steam of the workweek with a few drinks and a few turns on the dance floor...

I'd also like to give a shout-out to my editor, Barb Toth, who figuratively wipes my face and makes sure my buttons are buttoned and flies done up before sending me out into the world. She is a mistress of continuity and if you find any details at all that are wrong in the story, blame me and not her.

I'm also grateful to NineStar Press for giving me a vibrant and honest publishing home, one where I feel I'm truly part of the family.

Of course, no acknowledgments would be complete without mention of my family—my son, Nicholas, who inspired the character of Riccardo, and my husband, Bruce, whose undying love and support ground me and, at the same time, allow me that most important commodity for a writer, the time to dream.

Last, I thank you, dear reader, for collaborating with me in bringing this dream to life. I love working with you.

About Rick R. Reed

Real Men. True Love.

Rick R. Reed is an award-winning and bestselling author of more than fifty works of published fiction. He is a Lambda Literary Award finalist. *Entertainment Weekly* has described his work as "heartrending and sensitive." *Lambda Literary* has called him: "A writer that doesn't disappoint..." Find him at www.rickrreedreality.blogspot.com. Rick lives in Palm Springs, CA, with his husband, Bruce, and their fierce Chihuahua/Shiba Inu mix, Kodi.

Email
rickrreedbooks@gmail.com

Facebook
www.facebook.com/rickrreedbooks

Twitter
@rickrreed

Other NineStar books by this author

Also from NineStar Press

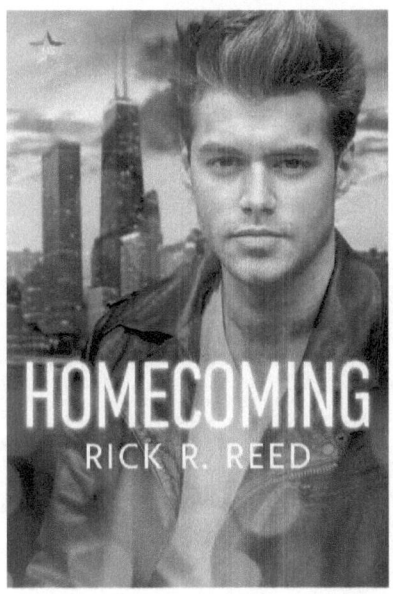

Homecoming by Rick R. Reed

After losing his partner Toby, Chase faces a long, painful road back to life and love.

At first, he doesn't see how he can go on, but then Chase and Toby's old friend Mike cajoles him into returning to Chicago for the annual International Mr. Leather Competition. There Chase revisits a world of hot, casual sex that he had forgotten existed, meets a friend who cares more for him than he ever realized, and discovers the possibility that he just might be able to move on without betraying the memory of his late partner.

Will Chase find his way back once more to life? To love? And will he find that place he's been missing? *Home.* You'll have to experience the heartrending journey firsthand to find out.

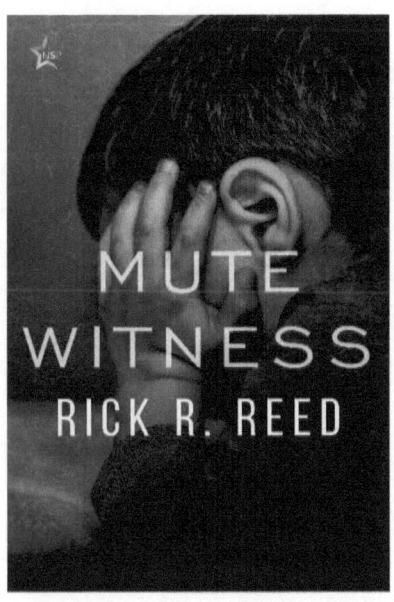

Mute Witness by Rick R. Reed

Sean and Austin have the perfect life. Their new relationship is only made more joyous by weekend visits from Sean's eight-year-old son, Jason.

And then their perfect world shatters.

Jason is missing.

When the boy turns up days later, he has been abused and has lost the power to speak. Small town minds turn to the boy's gay father and his lover as the likely culprits. Sean and Austin struggle to maintain their relationship amid the innuendo and the threat that Sean will lose the son he loves. Meanwhile, the real villain is close to home, intent on ensuring the boy's muteness is permanent.

Stranded with Desire by Rick R. Reed and Vivien Dean

CEO Maine Braxton and his invaluable assistant, Colby, don't realize they share a deep secret: they're in love—with each other. That secret may have never come to light but for a terrifying plane crash in the Cascade Mountains that changes everything.

In a struggle for survival, they brave bears, storms, and a life-threatening flood to make it out of the wilderness alive. The proximity to death makes them realize the importance of love over propriety. Confessions emerge. Passions ignite. They escape the wilds renewed and openly in love.

When they return to civilization, though, forces are already plotting to snuff out their short-lived romance and ruin everything both have worked so hard to achieve.

Connect with NineStar Press

www.ninestarpress.com

www.facebook.com/ninestarpress

www.facebook.com/groups/NineStarNiche

www.twitter.com/ninestarpress

www.instagram.com/ninestarpress